Driving
the Horse
in Harness

1. Lynn and Paul Likus of Annandale, New Jersey, out for an afternoon's drive behind their crossbred pony put to a wicker pony cart.

Driving
the Horse
in Harness

A BEGINNER'S MANUAL

by CHARLES W. KELLOGG

Editor of *The Whip*

Drawings by Karl Stuecklen

The Stephen Greene Press

BRATTLEBORO, VERMONT

TO Daphne, MY WIFE

without whose encouragement,
knowledge, research and enthusiasm, this project never
would have been completed!

This book has been produced in the United States of America.
It is designed by R. L. Dothard Associates and published by The Stephen Greene
Press, Brattleboro, Vermont 05301

LIBRARY OF CONGRESS CATALOGING IN PUBLICATION DATA

Kellogg, Charles W   1914–

  Driving the horse in harness.

  Bibliography: p.
  Includes index.

  1. Show driving of horse-drawn vehicles. I. Title.
SF305.7.K44 798'.6 77-92777
ISBN 0-8289-0332-8
ISBN 0-8289-0333-6 pbk.

Contents

Acknowledgments

Grateful acknowledgment is made to Judy Buck for photographs 26 and 27, reprinted from *The Morgan Horse Handbook* by Jeanne Mellin with the kind permission of the author; to A. V. Frost for 38 and 39; Taffy McKeon for 4; Robert Moseder for 45; James F. O'Rourke, Jr., for 25, 30–32 and 41; *Practical Horseman* magazine for 19–24 and 28; Serafin Sulky Company for 5; Elizabeth Shallow for 40; and *Western Horseman* magazine for 2. The remaining photographs are from the author's collection.

The publisher, for its part, would like to add a word of thanks to Sarah Swift of Brattleboro, a faithful font of information on all things horse—and to Tim Ragle of Guilford, who generously shared valuable source material with the editor.

A Reawakening:

an introduction

The horse and buggy era flourished in the United States for less than a century. Primitive roads held back wheeled travel in this country until well into the 19th century, while in the early days of the 20th the advent of the motor vehicle doomed the horse-drawn variety as a necessity of life and transportation.

Prior to World War I the majority of horses in this country were used in the transport of people and goods, and in agriculture. There were some sporting uses, of course, but the basic use of the horse was as a source of power. The internal combustion machine changed all that; with it, the horse-powered vehicle went into limbo.

However, after World War II the riding horse staged a comeback and by 1960 there were more horses in the United States than at any time in the previous 50 years. Hand-in-hand with this "explosion" in the general horse population came a considerable revival of interest in, and use of, horse-drawn carts and carriages—not as a necessary of life, but for sport and recreation.

Companionship surely played, and plays, a part. Generally one riding horse equals one rider: togetherness in the saddle is achieved only by having as many horses as there are people. This is true whether trail riding, competing in the show ring, riding to hounds or atop a polo pony. But consider the carriage: the smallest can usually hold two, many more carry four and some up to a dozen. Herein lies one of the many appeals of this steadily growing pastime— the sport of driving for pleasure.

In *Driving the Horse in Harness* we will outline many of the things one needs to know to find enjoyment driving a horse. To enjoy any sport one must do it well, or at least as well as one is able. There is more to driving a horse than simply picking up a rein in each hand and saying, "Giddap." And one must drive safely—for one's own sake and for the sake of others. Pointers on driving technique and safety are here for the looking—and an early look at the glossary of driving terms just beyond the last chapter will help the beginner feel at home in the harness horse world all the sooner.

Here, too, we will consider the vehicle and what the reader should know about finding and caring for the right one. It isn't easy. Horse-drawn vehicles can't be bought at the corner drug store. Once upon a time most big mail-order houses catalogued a whole line of carriages, and carriage-making flourished from New England to Omaha; today, to obtain the traditional vehicles once so numerous, one must either import prohibitively expensive carriages from abroad, or haunt the handful of annual carriage auctions—and, even when successful there, hours, weeks and months of careful restoration must follow. Fortunately, modern versions of the two-wheeled cart are now being manufactured in the United States again, as we shall see.

And consider the horse. When the revival of pleasure driving began in the late 1950's there were few light horses trained to drive available. The average riding horse was just that, and the few fine harness animals there were were used almost exclusively for show, chiefly in the Morgan and

Hackney breed show rings. Beyond that, trainers of driving horses were as scarce as the vehicles for the horses to pull, and harness-making was an almost forgotten art.

But today, things are changing. Trainers of driving horses are reappearing; so are harness makers. Equine publications are tuning in to the needs of the driving horseman and horsewoman, and to the news of driving events and driving people. Articles on restoration are being published, and books on the pleasures and how-tos of driving the horse in harness are being written.

C.W.K.
Kellington Farm
Sharon, Connecticut

1

The Right Horse

N O T A L L saddle horses make good driving horses, but chances are that the average pleasure horse used for such activities as trail riding, hunting and equitation competition can be trained to work adequately and safely between shafts.

For the purposes of this book we are basically concerned with the single horse or pony. As a start, the best place to look for your first driving horse is right in your own barn. The horse you've ridden happily for the past months or years may be just the horse to pull you and your passengers across the countryside, or in the novice divisions of today's mounting number of driving competitions.

USING PONIES

Many of today's adult whips (drivers) began their driving experience with a pony. This makes a lot of sense. Well-broken ponies are in good supply; their initial cost is less than that for a horse, as is their upkeep. The pony which has been outgrown by its youthful rider can be driven at length by an adult without the latter looking or feeling "too big," and without fear of damage to the pony: any healthy pony 12.0 hands or over (a hand—for any rank beginners among you—equals 4 inches) should be able to handle a cart with one or two adults aboard fairly easily. Ponies 13.0 and over generally can cover as much ground in a day's outing as a horse, although it may take the pony a little longer.

Point of information: both the American Horse Shows Association and the American Driving Society hold to the accepted standard that any animal under 14.2 is to be considered a pony. There are exceptions—the Morgan being one. A Morgan can compete as a horse regardless of size. This also applies to the Arab, Standardbred and Quarter Horse. However, under FEI (Fédération Équestre Internationale) rules—rules which apply to a number of driving events—any animal competing as a horse must be 14.2 or over.

Pony Breeds

The most popular pony breed used for driving has been the Welsh, either purebred or crossed with the Thoroughbred,

2. Amanda Pirie of Hamilton, Massachusetts, in a pony village cart behind a registered Welsh pony from her mother's Aquila Farm.

Arab, Hackney or Connemara. These mixes have size and substance, and are usually attractive.

Purebred Hackneys also do well in driving competitions, especially Hackneys with the blood of Cassilis Farm studs (the Cassilis Farm of New Marlboro, Massachusetts, is the oldest Hackney pony stud in continuous operation in the United States). However, these spirited ponies are not for beginners.

Lesser-known pony breeds of European origin—the Haflinger and the Connemara in particular—are also seen in the pleasure driving ranks.

To many, the Shetland seems a little small for extended cross-country tours, either for picnics or in competitions, but their owners often think otherwise, and in 1976 the Shetland Pony Association of America wrote its own rules for driving competitions.

THE DRIVING HORSE

As with the driving pony, there is no one "must" horse breed: the Morgan, Hackney, Standardbred and American Saddle Horse all have their champions, as do many others—including any number of crossbreds.

The Morgan

The merits of the Morgan horse as a driving animal cannot be denied. Working in harness is the Morgan's heritage. A big plus is the fact that almost all Morgan farms train their young stock to drive long before they begin their work under saddle, so the Morgan that doesn't drive is a rarity. But, whatever the reason, there is no doubt that Morgan numbers have been increasing rapidly in the pleasure driving world of late. Among the best of these have been the liver chestnuts bred and raised by Mr. and Mrs. J. Cecil

3. Looking very elegant, Margaret Ferguson Noyes driving a pair of her parents' Broadwell Farm Morgans put to a spider phaeton.

Ferguson at their Broadwell Farm in Greene, Rhode Island. The Broadwell Morgans, impeccably turned out, have been consistent winners as singles, pairs, unicorns (single leader and a pair of wheelers), and four-in-hands at such major shows as Devon and the Royal Winter Fair in Toronto.

The Standardbred

The basic unraced Standardbred horse has pleasure driving potential to a large degree. A good example is a smart little four-in-hand team owned by George A. Weymouth of Chadds Ford, Pennsylvania, now very active in the sport. His Standardbreds are driven to a three-quarter size roof seat break (a sporting vehicle drawn by a pair or four-in-hand), and are very quick and handy, as one would expect of horses barely 14.2. They won the four-in-hand division at Hamilton, Massachusetts, in 1975 against a number of bigger teams, including several teams of Canadian crossbreds and European imports. When not competing, their owner/

whip enjoys less formal driving than that required in the competitions. He revels in simpler drives through the lovely Brandywine countryside or in joining with other whips and their teams at sporting events such as hunt races, horse shows and polo matches—in the role of both country squire and spectator.

Another fine Standardbred four-in-hand team is that owned by John Jenkle of Sebastopol, California. This team was a familiar sight during the 1977 driving season when the Jenkles brought it all the way across the country, at considerable effort and with no little luck, to hit most of the driving-circuit high spots.

However, there are several problems attendant to Standardbreds as purely pleasure horses. Those animals of the breed which have been raced, or trained for racing, are often found to have very hard (slow to respond) mouths. Others suffer from the familiar ills of the race horse— unsoundness of hoof or leg, or the nervous afflictions of many stall-bound horses, such as cribbing, weaving and stall-walking.

The numbers of good Standardbreds available for the road are diminished even further by a system which sends the females back to the breeding farms once their best track days are over, while the males continue to race until well past their peak, moving down the ladder of track importance until they finally arrive at the sales ring. There they are often grabbed up by the Amish and Mennonites.

But the biggest factor in the lack of good Standardbreds for driving is that the majority of Standardbreds being trained and raced today are pacers, and this is a gait neither favored, nor indeed permitted, in carriage competitions. We have known owners to drive pacers happily enough on the open road, and many "sidewheelers" are seen on the roads of Amish communities, but the trot is a required gait in the ADS (American Driving Society) and FEI rule books.

ing field, and in the hunter-equitation show rings, so we are beginning to find these versatile horses between shafts. Their blocky hindquarters may not be considered ideal by carriage horse fanciers of long standing, and their flat-footed gaits, so desirable in the Western show ring, may seem dull in contrast to the more animated Morgan, but from a purely practical viewpoint, their calm dispositions and general hardiness make them highly suitable for pleasure driving.

The Thoroughbred

Owners of Thoroughbreds may feel left out of this driving horse review—and with some reason. The Thoroughbred is all that the name implies, but the natural inclination of the Thoroughbred to a low "grass-cutting" action is considered less attractive in harness—at least for competitive purposes. A trot, which must be the carriage horse's major gait, is not the Thoroughbred's—an animal for generations bred to run. But many have been versatile enough to learn and many Thoroughbreds are now being driven by their fond owners; in particular, put to sleighs and to country-style carts. There is no reason why the Thoroughbred cannot be a pleasure to drive providing the individual animal has the temperament for the job.

The Crossbred

However, in the hunt for a good driving horse, it is not necessary to look exclusively for a "driving breed," especially if purely pleasure driving is the immediate goal. The Hackney, the Standardbred, the Morgan and the Fine Harness horse all have their place in the sport, but there are more crossbreds by far being driven at present than there are purebreds.

For one thing, there are a great many horses in light harness today with draft-horse blood from the dam. One good example is Littlejohn, a Pinto–Belgian crossbred campaigned in driving competitions for many years by owner Angela Seibert of Millbrook, New York. By conformation standards Littlejohn is perhaps too chunky, and his spotted color turns some traditionalists off, but he has a good reaching trot, more than adequate stamina, powerful hindquarters and dogged determination. Little more can be asked of a driving horse and, in 1976, he scored a convincing victory in the FEI competitions at Hamilton, Massachusetts.

Critics have labeled the draft-blood crossbreds, most of them being imports from Canada, as being too big, clumsy and coarse, at least when compared to the purebred Morgan, American Saddle Horse or Standardbred: conformationwise they may have a point, but conformation isn't everything. Just as the Canadian-bred colt sired by a Thoroughbred out of a Percheron mare was imported to fill the need for middleweight and heavyweight hunters in the United States, so have the colts by Hackney sires out of Percheron and Clydesdale mares been imported to pull the heavier vehicles of English and Continental design so much in favor in pleasure driving today—many of these carriages calling for a horse approaching 16 hands or more.

Of course the crossbred Littlejohns are something of a rarity. There are very few spotted horses seen in carriage competitions, at least along the Eastern seaboard—perhaps due to the historic reluctance of the English-style rider and fox hunter to use spotted horses. Since the majority of horses being driven in the 70's began their careers under saddle one thing has seemingly led to the other.

In the East over the past ten years there has been a steady demand for the Hackney-on-draft crossbred. Bred for the most part in the Canadian provinces of Ontario and Quebec, where Hackneys are plentiful, they often are a "second crop" to the owners of draft mares being used on farms or in the production of medicinal fluids. Just as the market for heavyweight hunters in the United States encouraged Thoroughbred-on-draft matings, so has the new-found enthusiasm for driving opened a new outlet for the Hackney-on-draft offspring.

At Kellington Farm we have good examples of these. Our Kitchener and Kingston are a pair of bay geldings—15.3½ and 16.0 hands respectively, and 1,250 pounds each. They are by the same Hackney stallion out of French Coach mares, the latter being crossbreds themselves with some light draft blood. They have been driven single, pair, tandem, unicorn and four-in-hand as wheelers—and have done well.

Another good example of a successful crossbred is our Canadian Gamble. He is a grey gelding, 16.0 hands, 1,300 pounds, sired by a Thoroughbred stallion out of a grade Percheron mare. He was purchased as a suckling in Quebec, thus his name, with the idea that he would make a good combination horse—a hunter which could be driven. He was hunted lightly, as a staff horse with hounds, and was ridden in hunting pace events, but as we became more deeply involved in driving his primary duties changed. He has been a winner as a ladies' driving horse, has shared trophies with one of the above bays as a tandem leader, and works well with both bays as a unicorn leader and as near (left side) leader in a four-in-hand.

Canadian Kalamity, a bay mare, 16.0 hands, 1,050 pounds, is still another mix—by an Arab stallion out of a Clydesdale mare. She goes as a single, tandem wheeler (nearest the vehicle), and as unicorn and four-in-hand leader. So in that one team of four we have Hackney, Arab, Thoroughbred, Percheron, French Coach and Clydesdale blood. And they all go pretty well together.

This is not to say that all crossbreds make good driving

4. Canadian Gamble—by a Thoroughbred stallion out of a Percheron mare: a prime example of a crossbred driving horse—put to an East Williston cart during a dressage event and driven by Craig Kellogg, son of the author.

horses. There are many individual animals which prove that point only too well. But, during the 1970's, crossbreds were becoming more and more familiar on the driving scene, particularly among the coaching fraternity. For example, John C. Fairclough, a New Jersey sportsman who served as president of the Carriage Association of America in 1976–1977, drove a majestic team of black Hackney–Percheron geldings, and another four-in-hand of the same breeding, although somewhat lighter, was in the stables of Mr. and Mrs. James K. Robinson, Jr. of West Chester, Pennsylvania.

Four-in-hands are certainly not for everybody, *surely* not for the beginner. We have cited the above examples simply because they are impressive showpieces for the carriage sport, and to point up the fact that no one breed is required to make a potentially good driving horse.

What breed, then, is the driving horse? As we have seen,

the answer is *all* of those discussed here—and perhaps others. What we have tried to show is that there is no one "perfect" breed choice for driving—though, on careful consideration, the Morgan very probably comes closest.

FINDING THE HORSE

Where does the beginning whip search for his first driving horse? As we suggested earlier, perhaps the best place to look is in the family barn. But if the family barn turns up nothing, where to look next? The marketplace for horses in this country is a big one—and, for the beginner, a perilous one.

Two words of advice for anyone, but especially for the beginner: Stay as close to home as possible in your search and take an experienced and trusted horseman along with you. If you are set on a horse already trained to drive, at this writing there are, in this country, at least a good handful of professionals exclusively concerned with driving. Any one of them, or perhaps others you may find on your own, could give you the advice you need. A few queries in driving circles should help you find your man.

However, as we've said, it is not necessary to confine your search to a horse already trained in harness or to deal exclusively with these top specialists. There are other ways to go. If your own barn turned up nothing, look elsewhere for an everyday good riding horse—either to train yourself (this can be great fun and very satisfying, if you have the time and patience), or to have trained for you. There are far more riding horses than those trained to drive, making it considerably easier and less expensive to buy a quiet, well-mannered riding horse of decent age—an animal already exposed to the perils of traffic, the confusion of the show ring and the foibles of inexperienced handlers—than to buy a well-seasoned driving horse. Although first choice might best go to one of the breeds or crossbreds we've discussed above, once the usual tests for soundness and tractability have been met, there is no reason why almost any horse you select cannot be trained to work in harness.

Basically, what you want is the horse that the neighborhood gal is giving up as she goes off to college after many years on that horse's back. The outgrown pony in the next town might suit—or perhaps the seasoned hack not quite classy enough for the local professional hunting-boarding-equitation stable.

The Horse Sale

Another alternative is the horse sale, but here the buyer must be wary. Many of these sales advertise "driving horses," and no doubt a number of these are well-trained in harness, but a lifetime with horses has convinced me that I, for one, don't know enough to be turned loose at an auction sale and be sure I'll get home with the horse I thought I went to buy. Large-animal vets and tack shop personnel are good sources for information on the better auction sales; general information can usually be found in local newspapers and of course in the special locally-oriented horse publications. But remember: this is where the beginner will want the company of a highly experienced horseman.

If money is no object, breed sales are another alternative. Once in a while good "bargains" can be picked up at breed farms: these farms occasionally have "leftovers"—mares who won't breed, geldings that didn't sell, or a less-perfect product—that they will sell quite reasonably. But here, too, the beginner needs the company of someone with a good eye for horseflesh. Look to the breed magazines for information about these sales.

And a final word: no matter the source, beginners should steer clear of stallions. They are just too tricky.

Costs

It is difficult to give a good rule-of-thumb as to what the new convert to driving should have to pay for his pleasure: ponies will be cheaper than horses; prices vary by season and locale, and of course by bloodline. But although one can pay as much as $3,500 for a top-quality driving animal, a careful hunt should be able to turn up a perfectly adequate animal for as little as $750 or even less.

"Style" vs Conformation

In the days when horse power was the only power available to move one along the roads and streets of the country, "style" was often *the thing*. We are not so preoccupied nowadays. There are few formal carriages being driven, and when we do see them—generally in parades, pageants and the like—the horses often are completely "wrong" as far as tradition is concerned. Our forefathers would have cringed at the sight of a Brougham pulled by a pair of Belgians, or a horse-sized Victoria being dragged about by 13.0-hand ponies; today, only the purists would care.

The current revival in pleasure driving centers around the pleasure carriage and the sporting vehicle rather than the formal park or city carriage, and the horse or pony used should be one with the proper conformation to do the job. The cross-country horse should be able to do just that—go across a piece of country, much in the way of the hunting horse without the need to jump, but with the shoulders and hindquarters and depth of girth to give him the strength to pull a carriage and passengers for a given time at a constant rate of speed. Further, he (or she) should have good feet, for much of today's travel must be on paved roads.

Beyond this, today's pleasure driving horse should fit his carriage. This is more a matter of pleasing the eye than concern over burdening the beast with too heavy a load. On the road, "fit," in the sense of relating horse to vehicle, is less important than in some of the competition classes where a certain percentage of the judging is based on "suitability," or "fit," of horse to carriage. Although not of particular importance to the beginner, this matter of "suitability" gains importance as one's driving experiences broaden.

2

The Two-Wheelers

U N L E S S Y O U happen to be one of the few lucky people who have a cache of antique carriages hidden away in an old barn somewhere, the selection and purchase of your first vehicle is a crucial step toward the enjoyment of your driving horse. There are several important considerations.

If you are a beginning driver and/or your horse is newly trained in harness, it is recommended that your first vehicle be a two-wheeled cart. These are lighter than the four-wheeled vehicles, they are less expensive, and most of all, they are much safer.

The young or green horse just cannot always be trusted to go forward in a straight line, no matter how willingly he has taken to the tasks asked of him in harness. A sudden turn or back-up when the horse might be frightened is much easier to handle if you have only two wheels to worry about at the same time you are coping with the animal. The same situation in a four-wheeled vehicle often results in a cramping of the front wheels against the side of any carriage which is not "cut-under" (an arch in the body of the carriage into which the wheels can turn more freely), and

16

problems can develop even with one having a "full lock" (construction allowing an almost 360 degree turn).

A broken shaft is the least of the possible unpleasant results; worse, the carriage can overturn, throwing out driver and passengers. This can lead to a thoroughly frightened horse, his original fright now compounded by the mess behind him. A frantic horse still attached to an overturned carriage becomes extremely difficult to control as he fights to get away from it all, with more injury to animal, people and vehicle quite likely—a development to be avoided if at all possible. Not only is the immediate situation serious, but such accidents often result in a very skittish horse, one apprehensive of shafts and carriages for a long time, if not always.

On the other hand, the construction of the two-wheeled cart allows sudden turns without upset; the vehicle just pivots with the horse. In its turn, the unexpected back-up, while somewhat unpleasant, involves no cramping and the danger of being overturned is lessened greatly. Furthermore, it is just plain easier to drive a cart than a four-wheeled carriage. Let's take one example: an unexpected obstruction met in the road necessitates turning around. A horse drawing a two-wheeled vehicle can be turned around almost in its own length; in the same situation a four-wheeled carriage requires more room and perhaps a back-up of some distance. Backing up a four-wheeled vehicle with a green horse calls for a skill rarely seen in the beginning driver.

The main objection to the two-wheeler is that the most commonly used styles allow only limited passenger space. There are, however, somewhat more sophisticated antique types, such as the "dog" cart, which provide seats for four adults back to back, and there are the horse-sized tub carts which seat four adults riding sideways face to face in the style of the more familiar "governess" carts so often seen pulled by a pony. We'll have more about these carts as we go along.

THE NEW CARTS

Granted that the two-wheeled vehicle is the answer for the beginning driver, there is still the question of which cart— one of the simpler new wire- or wooden-wheeled versions or one of the favored, time-honored antique models?

If at all possible, the new driver should look to one of the simpler new models now on the market: they are sturdier, often easier to drive, and in the long run almost always cheaper, especially when the money and time involved in restoring a possibly damaged antique vehicle is considered.

Wire Wheel or Wooden?

Traditionalists frown upon modern carts with bicycle-type wire wheels; in fact, they are prohibited from most carriage shows and competitions, except in some instances where they are permitted for children and novice drivers. They are, however, encouraged, if not required, in the breed show rings. For pleasure driving they can accommodate one adult and one child with some comfort, but they lack a sturdy back rest which can be tiring on a long cross-country haul.

But the wire-wheeled, often called "jog," carts have much merit. They are light and can be moved around easily by women or children. They put relatively little weight on the shoulders of a young or small horse. They are also very sturdy. Since they are new they need no restoration. Beyond that, they are readily available since several firms make and market them: Serafin Sulky Co., Stafford Springs, Connecticut; and Jerald Sulky Co., 3050 Wagner Rd., Waverly, Iowa; are two of these. Best of all is the fact

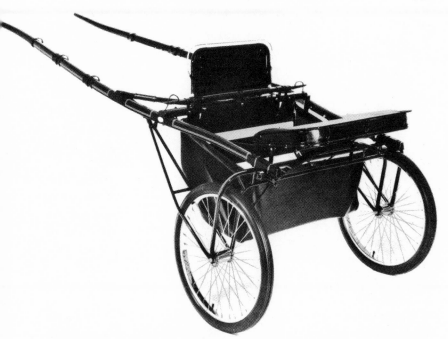

5. A Serafin two-passenger pleasure jog cart. It features a full-width Whiffle (or single)-tree and heavy duty wheels. The shafts are of white ash, the arch and forks of tubular steel.

that these carts can be used for training and exercising, and for other rough work, without risking the much more expensive antique carts to damage by a green horse or an inexperienced whip. The costs for these wire-wheeled carts vary, but range from perhaps $1,200 for a *new* rubber-tired horse-sized model to a minimum of $700 for a simpler pony model. With luck, secondhand wire-wheeled carts are sometimes available—at a somewhat lower price tag.

Mainly in order to fill the need for a fairly simple competition cart with wooden wheels, several modern carts designed after the traditional carts of old have recently appeared. Generally manufactured to order, these carts do seat two adults comfortably, have a back rest, rubber tires, and meet the requirements for cross-country competition. Priced in roughly the same range as the bicycle-wheeled version, they also make a very satisfactory vehicle for the green horse and the neophyte whip.

BREAKING CARTS

Anyone training a driving horse—neophyte and veteran whip alike—should have access to a so-called breaking cart. Several types of breaking carts can be found. Some are of recent construction, some are antique. They feature an elongated floor which extends backwards from the very plain body. With handholds at either side of the simple plank seat (for one or two), the design allows the trainer to stand on the back of the cart, mounting or dismounting easily by stepping up or down six inches or so.

Most breaking carts are built of sturdy wood on very spartan lines and are relatively inexpensive. They *can* be used as a pleasure cart, but their cross-country use is somewhat limited by the low-slung floor which is apt to drag on the ground when used over uneven terrain. You'll find a picture of a breaking cart in use in the harnessing sequence in Chapter 4.

A more elaborate version is the "Kentucky" breaking cart—already familiar as a pleasure vehicle and offering more comfort to the driver and passenger. These are antique, larger and a bit heavier than the basic cart already described, probably due to the fact that they originated in Kentucky for use with the American Saddle Horse, Tennessee Walker and other sturdy Mid-South breeds.

THE OLD FAVORITES

But practicality for the beginner and breed-show requirements aside, the favored two-wheeled driving vehicle is now, and likely will remain, the familiar antique driving cart of earlier manufacture. Some of the favorites of these, and tips on where and how to buy them, follow.

Finding the Oldies

Antique wooden-wheeled vehicles can be found at the secondhand sales at widely varying prices—anywhere, say, from $400 to $1,500, and sometimes much more. But, of course, they require considerable restoration effort—thus the reluctance to risk them to inexperienced whips and horses for everyday driving.

One of the best places to find the antique vehicles is at Martin Auctioneers of Blue Ball, Pennsylvania, which runs semi-annual carriage auctions, usually in May and August. In recent years, another auction has been held in Springfield, Massachusetts, in July. Smaller private sales are also held from time to time.

As the interest in driving increases, chances are that the number of public auctions will also increase; those interested should keep their eyes open for news of these in the various horse-interest media and their ears open for such news among fellow drivers.

BUYER BEWARE

When buying antique vehicles—whether the two-wheeled carts we are talking about in this chapter, or the more extensive and expensive vehicles we'll talk about in the next chapter—there are very important practical things to look out for. Be sure to check the crucial metal for signs of wear. The crucial metal includes the springs and reach (the longitudinal supporting member between the front and back axles of some four-wheeled carriages); the rest is ornamental. At the same time, test the wood for signs of rot. This

6. Owner Angela Seabrook driving her versatile Littlejohn put to a Meadowbrook cart.

can be done carefully and considerately with a small penknife.

Some veterans we have talked with prefer to buy only unfinished pieces: They feel that once a vehicle has been painted it is more difficult to evaluate. And this is a good spot to remind new owners of antique vehicles to turn to the last chapter in *Driving the Horse in Harness* for tips on whatever restoration may be necessary.

Long Island Carts

The most sought-after of the antique two-wheeled vehicles during the current driving for pleasure revival has been the group now lumped together under the heading of "Long

Island utility" carts. Named for the location of their manufacture rather than for any minute design deviation, they are the East Williston cart, the Meadowbrook cart, the Hempstead cart and the Mineola cart. A similar cart, manufactured and marketed in West Chester, Pennsylvania, is identified by that name.

The Long Island group makes an ideal pleasure vehicle for all classes of drivers. The cart is entered from the rear by stepping on a low platform, thence through a fold-up seat which lifts easily to give access to the driving and passenger positions. They have a low center of gravity and a unique system of springs which make the "ride" soft and pleasurable, and high wooden wheels with either iron or rubber tires. Made in several sizes, they are attractive in appearance. Seldom painted, their natural wood finish—with brown leather trim—gives them a sporting look; when fitted with a polished brass rein rail, brass shaft tips and the like, they sparkle. We'll call your attention to some of these Long Island carts in the captions for various of the photographs throughout the book.

The "East Williston" cart was born in the Long Island town of that name about 1890 and proved popular at once. Far from an "elegant" vehicle, it was nevertheless used for almost all but most formal outings, and by ladies as well as men. A groom might on occasion take the passenger's seat to assist a lady whip, but livery was out of place here, and a simple breast-collar harness (more about that later, too) was held most suitable. These carts retained their popularity long after the advent of the automobile, and are still relatively plentiful today among the antiques being restored and used. They are acceptable under all competition rules now in effect.

The Family Cart

"Moving up" from the simpler carts we've already discussed comes about almost inevitably as your horse gains more experience and you become more proficient as a driver. Chances are you will want to broaden your driving activity—in one or more of several directions—and you will need a more versatile vehicle, or vehicles, to accomplish this. Now is the time to select the direction you are heading first.

If you are primarily concerned with fun for the whole family your choice of two-wheeled vehicle is quite limited, since only a few will seat more than the driver and one passenger. (We'll, of course, look at good four-wheel possibilities when we get to that in the next chapter.)

Dog Carts

One two-wheeled cart which can accommodate four people is the "dog" cart, some of which are also known as "going to cover" carts. They were so named from their use to carry hunting dogs—the dogs tucked in a compartment under the passengers' seats, with louvres on the sides to provide the dogs with air. Considerably higher off the ground than the Long Island group, and thus with a somewhat higher center of gravity, the dog carts seat their human load back to back.

7. A dog cart. The dog cart continues to be a popular general-purpose cart, made in many variations. Most accommodated four, including the whip, in a back-to-back seating arrangement. The slatted box beneath the rear seat served as a carrier for hunting dogs.

The accompanying diagram will give you a good idea.

Most of the dog carts are equipped with mechanical devices designed to move the seats forward or backward as necessary to maintain the weight directly over the axle, thus avoiding undue pressures on the horse's back and harness. The original dog carts were painted, carried lamps and were rather more elegant than the East Willistons and their ilk. A more formal black harness was, and is, usual in polite dog-cart society.

Village Carts

Then there are the "village" carts, several varieties of them. Both in this country and abroad these carts were designed as utility vehicles, whether used in town or country. Some were painted in bright colors; some retained their natural wood finishes. Though most of them have very limited space for passengers, some versions are built with a back seat and a four-adult capacity. The Whitechapel cart is very similar. There are several examples of village carts pictured later in the book.

Show Ring Carts

Should your wishes lead you toward the more formal confines of the show ring rather than toward the informality of the open road, you will want a different type of vehicle.

Gigs

In the two-wheeled category, a "gig" might be your choice. These hold only two people, but of course have the advantage of two-wheel flexibility. Among the most popular of these are the Stanhope and Tilbury gigs. A Tilbury is shown

8. A Tilbury gig. Gigs were light, rather elegant two-wheelers seating two facing forward.

in Figure 8. Both were designed and commissioned by the Honorable Fitzroy Stanhope early in the 19th century. Painted, and considerably more formal than most American-inspired two-wheeled carts, the Stanhope calls for a Hackney or other type of "high stepper" between its curved shafts, and more formal dress to match. For many years the Stanhope was looked upon as a vehicle for a man rather than a lady, though perhaps this is not so true today.

A TWO-WHEELER RECAP

By now it should be clear that the two-wheeled driving vehicle has a number of specific uses, at the same time encompassing a wide range of driving activity very satisfactorily indeed. Beginning with the needs for safety *and* ease of handling for the beginner, as well as lower cost; through the early stages of competition and use as an informal road vehicle; and leading eventually to more formal experiences, the many fine two-wheelers are an integral part of driving for pleasure.

There are perfectly good two-wheeled carts that we have not, chiefly in interest of space and time, discussed in this chapter—the ralli and governess, for instance. At the same time we have avoided discussion of such exotic vehicles as the cocking and tandem carts, as these carts should be driven only by the very skillful.

As we have seen, the two-wheeled cart is available in new models with both wire and wooden wheels at modern carriage makers and in antique wooden-wheeled models, chiefly at the secondhand sales—with costs ranging from perhaps $400 to $1,500 for the new models and up to perhaps $1,000 for the antique models.

However, if there is one single point that we would like to have remembered from this chapter, it is that the two-wheeled cart is the *ideal*, if not the *only* proper, vehicle for the beginning whip, the beginning horse—and both!

3

The Four-Wheelers

A S W E have seen, in the current driving boom, where the emphasis centers around the single horse, and especially for the beginning whip, two-wheeled vehicles predominate—mainly because of their maneuverability, but also because of their availability. However, on the roadways, where cross-country driving is so popular these days, and in many show rings, four-wheeled vehicles are now very familiar; and once two or more horses are harnessed, the four-wheeler becomes a necessity—unless you are one of the very few to own such exotic pieces as the two-wheeled "curricle" or the "Cape" cart of South African origin.

Anyhow, let's say that you have made the decision, for whatever reason, to move up to a four-wheeler. Unfortunately, that decision is only the beginning: choosing, among the many, which type of four-wheeler would best suit your needs and then finding it, or its close approximation, at a price you can afford is rarely easy. And, of course, the process doesn't end there: careful and painful restoration must often follow.

The choice of four-wheeled vehicles is wide—and confusing. Many seasoned driving aficionados cannot keep them

9. Edward C. Dukehart of Madonna, Maryland, driving his hunter put to a four-wheeled trap at the 1977 Milady's picnic drive.

straight so the beginning driver should not feel too at sea if it takes a while to sort it all out. For the purposes of this book, we'll touch lightly on the development of the four-wheelers and suggest a few styles that might work best for most. For those interested in a deeper study, a look at the bibliography at the end of the book will point the way to some good source material. And, in addition to the reading material there, the restoration chapter points the way to several of the excellent museums featuring extensive carriage collections. A visit to one or more of these splendid museums will prove both a mine of information on the ve-

hicles themselves *and* a treat not many driving fans will want
to put off too long.

A LITTLE HISTORY

Without going into a detailed discussion of vehicle construction, the major difference between American and foreign
carriages over the years was not found in the design or
craftsmanship but in the wood: hickory, locust, ash and elm
provided American manufacturers with materials stronger
and much lighter than the woods native to England and the
European continent. The smaller American horses made
good use of the lighter vehicles, and some proof of the
American superiority thus afforded is seen in the fact that,
by the later years of the 19th century, European carriages
were rolling on wheels exported from America.

However, in "elegance," American carriage construction
remained second to that of the leading British and European manufacturers. There were a few notable exceptions—Brewster, French & Company and Flandreau, for
example.

The designers of the lighter American one-horse and pair
carriages seem to have had a disdain for sharp corners.
Whether or not this was due to the relatively more open
spaces of the American continent, as compared to the
smaller scale of the English and European landscape and
roads, is not explained. But it is well known that the streets
in American cities and towns were roomier than the tight
hedge-bordered lanes of the British Isles and western
European countries.

Many American-made carriages did indeed have the
cut-under feature of the continental designs to permit
easier turns at right angles, or were built with smaller
wheels in front which allowed them to pass under the body,
but most of the buggies did not have these features, nor did

most of the surreys. Many of today's drivers avoid these latter carriages for just this reason. But appearances are deceiving, as we shall see in the discussion following.

THE BUGGY

In the United States the basic four-wheeled vehicle in the horse and buggy age was, of course, the "buggy."

Before the buggy there were the springless wagon and the chaise of "one hoss shay" fame. Heavier carriages, of English design for the most part, were familiar in the eastern American cities in the early days of the 19th century, but it was the buggy, with its rudimentary springing and simple body which connected the budding cities through the rough tracks and byways of those early days. And its popularity never waned in the back country of the nation where many can still be found in active use today. They were strictly utilitarian, like the American buckboard, and far from elegant, but they made their mark on the transportation scene, even much as the Model T Ford was to do in the late stages of the horse and buggy era.

The name "buggy" is not American in origin; in fact, it is said to have stemmed from the Hindi language of India where a two-wheeled vehicle, covered by a sunshade, was known as a "bag," pronounced "bug." How the name was brought to the western world and then to America to be applied to the most distinctive American carriage hasn't been recorded. Regardless, the American buggy became the most popular one-horse vehicle ever produced. It was the "jack-of-all-trades" among carriages, and was mass-produced on the early assembly lines of the forerunners of today's automobile industry. Just about every carriage manufacturer made a buggy, and just about every mail-order house sold them. In 1908, Sears, Roebuck listed 19 different models of the buggy, plus dozens of road wagons and

10. A buggy. This popular American driving vehicle was generally hung on two elliptic springs with a small perch in the center of the undercarriage. The buggy was usually driven to a single horse and sometimes sported the folding hood.

runabouts almost indistinguishable from the buggy. Even the famous carriage makers, Brewster & Company of Broome Street in New York City built what looked and rode like a buggy, though they called them runabouts or road wagons.

All of these were meant for use with one or two light horses and had a single seat for two people. They were extremely light, weighing less than 500 pounds, but nevertheless extraordinarily strong. Some had a hood which folded back in good weather, and forward in bad. (As it happens, hooded buggies have caused some confusion in the driving community: a common mistake among driving people today is to call any hooded vehicle a "doctor's buggy." In reality, the true doctor's buggy was of deeper construction and the hood extended further toward the horse than it did on most buggies—to give the doctor, and often his patient, maximum protection from the weather.)

Although, as we have said, most of the buggies did not have the cut-under feature (the body box making an arch into which the front wheels could pass when making a turn), some did. However, even those buggies which didn't have this feature didn't pose much problem: Their narrow bodies (23 inches was the standard body-box width of the buggies made for Sears, Roebuck in 1908) and tracks of at least 52 inches and some as wide as 62 inches combined to allow them to be turned without trouble in almost all normal circumstances, though admittedly not quite so tightly as those with the cut-under feature.

There were many varied springing styles, each manufacturer having his own little quirk of design enabling him to call a buggy by any other name of his choice. For example, the runabout, a streamlined version of the buggy, is also known as a road wagon and has many fond owners. For a little background on springing, see the accompanying *Springing* insert.

The Concord Buggy

The plainest of the plain was the Concord buggy which may well have been the forerunner of most American horse-driven vehicles. Records show that they were seen on the rough tracks and turnpikes across America well before the Civil War. Secondhand Concord buggies can be found at the secondhand sales for as little as $400—not too high a price tag for such a rugged and versatile vehicle.

It is true that buggies offer little inducement as far as passenger space goes, but it should be noted that buggy seats are wider than the box by six inches or more, thus

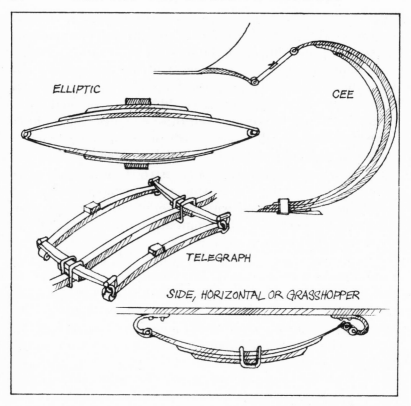

ELLIPTIC

CEE

TELEGRAPH

SIDE, HORIZONTAL OR GRASSHOPPER

11. Springing. Here are four examples of the many methods of carriage suspension employed over the years. The earliest springing was by leather braces with the body of the vehicle hung on straps attached to four pillars on the undercarriage. The telegraph springs (middle left) were an early improvement. They combined four double-elbow springs, two positioned laterally and two fore-and-aft; these, in turn, attached to the axle and the body. Later the whip spring, and its close relative, the cee (upper right), allowed a better ride but still required a vehicle perch (the longitudinal member running from front to rear axle around which the vehicle was built). In the early 1800's the elliptic spring (upper left) with the upper spring joined to the body and the lower to the axle, made the perch unnecessary, thus allowing a lighter and more elegant vehicle.

permitting two adults to sit side by side without too much crowding. The small narrow box behind cannot accommodate much more than a single package or box of groceries, or perhaps a picnic hamper for two—which is certainly all the human load the buggy should be asked to carry. So, not all drivers will be happy with a buggy: some will want a roomier, cut-under vehicle. *Nevertheless*, beginning drivers who wish to graduate from the "jog" cart to an inexpensive four-wheeled vehicle might well consider the buggy: it is a wonderfully utilitarian, and readily available, driving vehicle.

THE SURREY

The musical comedy "Oklahoma" featured a song extolling the joys of courting in a "surrey with a fringe on top." The words are descriptive, but the terminology is inaccurate. More correctly, the vehicle in question is a "canopy-top surrey," a term admittedly a little too difficult for a lyricist, and surely not so picturesque. "Fringe," "canopy," or whatever, there are a lot of surreys being seen in the current driving revival—and they do make a gay addition to the scene.

The four-wheeled surrey is an adaptation of the British "Whitechapel" cart's design, although modified considerably, and holds four adults in two seats, all facing forward. Basically the British body was lifted off its running gear and placed on a four-wheeled undercarriage much like that of the buggy, but heavier. It shares the narrow body of the buggy, but never was as popular. Yankee thrift may have played some role in this: the added cost for a surrey with a tunnel for the front wheels under the driver's seat was an average 10 percent more than for the same vehicle with straight sides. The design of the buggy allowed a little more flexibility in operation without such a tunnel.

12. A surrey. Some offered "the fringe on the top," others a fold-back top.

THE BUCKBOARD

Another early vehicle still visible is the buckboard. Buckboards—with a varying capacity up to nine adults—are as American as mother and apple pie. The earliest appeared in the first years of the 1800's and were little more than a seat set on three springy boards hung between two sets of wheels front and back. In the mid-1800's the pioneering firm of Jobert & White of Glens Falls, New York, began the manufacture of a refined version, some with eliptical springs and others with the sidebar or platform style springs. Buckboards found a wide acceptability from coast to coast, and were especially in favor in the Old West, and on the plains, because of their recognizably

American qualities—strength, simplicity, lightness of construction, and comfort for traveling over the rough roads and trails of frontier and rangeland.

THE PHAETONS

The largest grouping of carriages is found under the heading of "phaeton." This really describes a class of carriage rather than any distinct type. The name comes from Greek mythology; Phaeton was the son of Helios and famed for driving chariots across the sky. Just about every carriage manufacturer in the western world made a phaeton at some point, and many times one bore no resemblance at all to the next. In time, the term became familiarly applied to almost any four-wheeled vehicle generally driven by the owner or a non-professional.

In phaetons, there was no box for the coachman. Many had bodies made partly of wicker and these became known as "basket" phaetons. Carriages made especially for ladies—featuring ease of entering and leaving in flowing skirts, and parasols mounted behind and over the seats—naturally became known as "ladies' " phaetons. There were "morning" phaetons and "gentlemen's" phaetons, and Jobert & White even came out with a "buckboard" phaeton.

Not to be confused with the class of vehicle described above is the "George IV" phaeton, the first of which was made for that lame and sickly British king. An elegant carriage, sometimes called "a Victoria with the coachman's box removed," the George IV was low slung and easy for an invalid to get in and out of. It soon became the favorite of lady whips in the parks and on the city avenues, although the small front wheels lessened its use on the rougher roads of the countryside.

Today we find numerous phaetons in use for pleasure

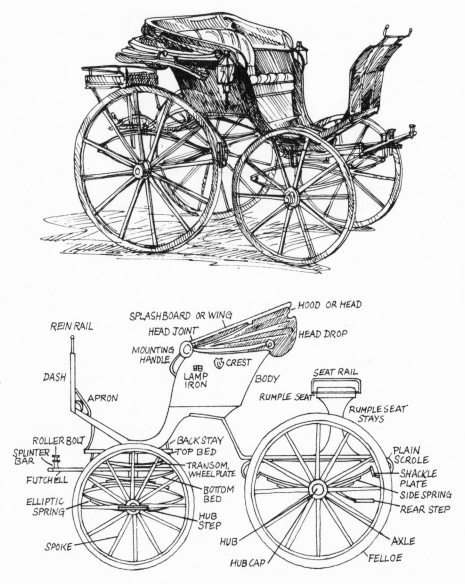

13. A spider phaeton. The spider phaeton featured a gig-shaped body, seating two, with a rumble seat for a groom.

driving—ranging from the simple wicker types favored by owners of ponies to the more elegant gentlemen's vehicles. As the style becomes more sophisticated, the number of pieces found diminishes, quite probably because they were more expensive in their own time with consequently fewer made, and also because so many of them were English made to begin with. (Although there is still a healthy trade in British carriages in this country, with at least one firm—M. J. Knoud, 716 Madison Avenue, New York City—importing them on a regular basis, British carriages by no means represent a majority of the carriages in use in this country.)

Still another form of phaeton we find in use today is the "trap" which requires the passengers riding on the second, or rear, seats to enter via the front of the vehicle, with one or more of the front seats being folded back to allow passage.

The accompanying spider phaeton drawing and the occasional phaetons pictured throughout the book give the reader a fair notion of this much-favored driving vehicle.

FOR TWO OR MORE HORSES

So far in this chapter we have dealt only with the pleasure and sporting types of carriage—and only those suitable for use with the single horse or pony, though most of them can be adapted for use with a pair by the simple substitution of a pole for the shafts. The emphasis here has been on the owner-driven vehicle to be enjoyed without coachmen or servants, even though many of the phaetons carried "jump" seats in the rear for use by a groom when wanted.

Beyond these, there are the more massive, and much more expensive, "breaks" and "wagonettes," suitable for from two to four horses. Also in this category are the drags and coaches of the royal and wealthy—the larger drags and

coaches requiring the grooms, guards, etc. considered a
necessity when driving more than a pair. Despite their size,
some of these more elegant carriages are viable for use in
today's driving revival, and are, indeed, being used—some
for fun, some for show, and some for commercial purposes.
This chapter, for example, shows a break very much in action.

In Earlier Days

The carriage era in its heyday featured many more vehicles
than we would have space to discuss here. There was a
whole world of closed and formal carriages, most of which
were used in town rather than in the country. One of the
most popular was the "Rockaway," of American origin. This
carriage, owned by many middle-class families, could carry
four to six passengers inside a body enclosed by glass, or
glass and curtains, the roof and side curtains extending
forward to protect the driver. The latter could be any male
member of the household, but most often was the all-
around "man" of the place, taken from his gardening or
maintenance chores to drive the lady of the house on a
shopping trip or social outing.

A rather more stylish carriage used for much the same
purposes, but always driven by a coachman, often in livery,
was the "Brougham." This particular carriage came into use
in England in the first half of the 19th century as a public
hack, but got its name and popularity as a private carriage
when Lord Brougham had one made for his own use. Generally a Brougham carried only two adults although many
had small folding seats for the small fry. The coachman sat
on a raised box unprotected from the weather; this in contrast to the roofed-over driver's area of the Rockaways. Carriage buffs tell us that Rockaways outnumbered Broughams
10-to-1 in America. No wonder.

"Victorias" and "vis-a-vis" carriages were "convertibles" with folded hoods which could be raised to protect the passengers from sun or rain. They were not sporting carriages in the true sense, being coachman-driven from the box, but were very fashionable for a drive in the park or on the avenue. Servants in livery were a *must* for these carriages, as they were for the even more formal "Landau" of German origin. The latter also had a folding roof, sat four people facing each other, was staffed by liveried servants, and is still seen today in ceremonies of state.

In the United States today, some Rockaways and Broughams remain in use, mainly in parades, or for such nostalgic events as driving newlyweds away from the church. They have little place in the sport of driving for pleasure, and are most familiar in museums or in the more elaborate amusement parks.

BUYING THE FOUR-WHEELER

Since it can cost up to and over $12,000 to buy a competition four-in-hand piece directly from the manufacturer in England and American manufacturers are only just beginning to make four-wheeled vehicles again, the best source for four-wheeled vehicles of all sizes and refinement continues to be the secondhand sales we talked about in the two-wheeler chapter.

As we saw earlier in this chapter a pared-down Concord buggy can be found at these sales for as little as $400; other more sophisticated carriages can range up to $1,500, and well over.

And remember—when selecting four-wheelers, the same two-wheeler safety rules apply: check the crucial metal (reach and springs) for wear and the wood for rot. Remember, too, to turn to the end of the book for our chapter on restoration hints.

4

Harnessing

T H E   B E G I N N I N G driver can get in trouble before he ever sits down behind his horse simply by buying a cheap harness.

The word "cheap" in this case is meant to describe a used harness which has been left hanging in a barn, cellar or loft since the horse which wore it last—generally several decades before—was led away for the last time. These often turn up at auctions, some are found in antique barns, some are advertised in the classified sections of equine periodicals and some in the "For Sale" columns of weekly newspapers in rural areas. And some belong to well-meaning friends who should know better.

Old, used harness is a safety risk, no matter how cheap the price. Unused for who knows how long, chances are the leather has deteriorated to the point it is no longer sound or safe. Harness must be cared for constantly: it cannot be hung up and left, nor can it be stored away in a trunk and forgotten. And once allowed to dry out in whatever place it has been stored, it can never be restored to its proper strength. Even new harness, unless constantly oiled and cleaned, can become dried out and unsafe.

Further, it is next to impossible to find used harness without worn places, pieces missing and buckles which don't match. It takes an expert horseman to find and buy a used harness worth the money paid for it; certainly this is a dangerous course for the unknowing beginner. We can hardly urge strongly enough that the beginning driver, unless he has the advantage of knowing a harness expert who can help find a decent used harness, would do well to buy a new one instead.

WHAT TO GET AND WHERE

The harness the beginner should have consists of a bridle with bit, driving reins, one of two types of check rein, a breast collar, harness saddle and girth, back strap, crupper and breeching with straps. In addition, if the horse is to be put to one of the beginning two-wheeled carts we discussed in chapter 2, a hold- or tie-down strap will be needed. See the harnessing diagrams on pages 44–45 for a better idea of what these harness parts look like and where they go.

A good source of new, safe, and inexpensive harness suitable for the beginning driver who plans to drive a single horse, to a simple vehicle strictly for his own enjoyment—at least in the beginning—are the harness shops of the "Plain People," the Amish and Mennonites of Pennsylvania, Ohio, Illinois, Wisconsin, Iowa and Canada. Many of the towns in these areas have Amish harness makers: Arcola, Illinois; La Grange, Indiana; Hazelton, Iowa; and Intercourse, Pennsylvania, are only four of many that come to mind.

There is nothing elegant about Amish-made harness: it is strictly utilitarian with no frills. But it is sound, will stand rather hard treatment, and is not costly. The cost of the "standard" Amish harness described below averages about $130. And, although it can be made to order (the Stoltzfus Shops in Intercourse and Leola, Pennsylvania, will do this), another great plus is that it can be bought right off the racks.

The standard Amish-made harness is of black leather with reins which are black at the bit end, but of russet

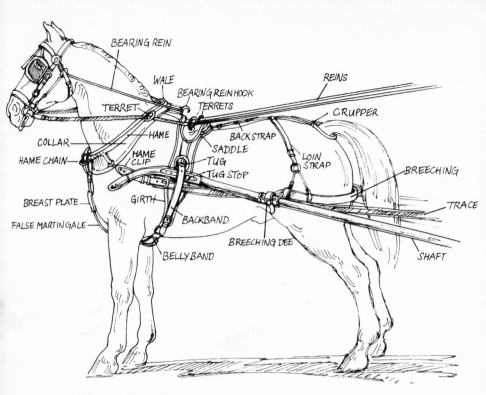

BEARING REIN

WALE

BEARING REIN HOOK
TERRETS

REINS

TERRET

CRUPPER

COLLAR

HAME

HAME CHAIN

HAME
CLIP

SADDLE

BACKSTRAP

TUG

LOIN
STRAP

TUG STOP

BREECHING

BREAST PLATE

GIRTH

BACKBAND

TRACE

FALSE MARTINGALE

BREECHING DEE

BELLY BAND

SHAFT

14. (*Above and opposite*). Details of single harness with round collar.

leather in the hands section. This is the harness which can usually be purchased over the counter (off the rack) at many harness shops. If the beginner has selected a cart or carriage of natural wood finish, he or she may wish to have a complete harness made of russet leather, which fades to a kind of tan; this color is considered more suitable than black for show or competition purposes. Russet harness is seldom stocked in Amish shops since it is forbidden for their own people, but some Amish and Mennonite harness makers will build russet harness on order. Also, the usual, plainer nickel hardware of the ordinary Amish harness can be replaced with brass, if desired.

If your horse is 14.2 and over, most stock Amish-made harness will adjust to fit him or her properly. A considerably out-sized animal might need specially ordered harness.

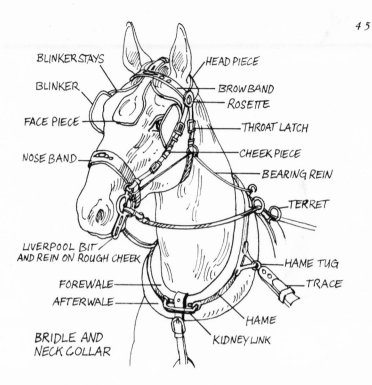

BLINKER STAYS

BLINKER

FACE PIECE

NOSE BAND

LIVERPOOL BIT
AND REIN ON ROUGH CHEEK

FOREWALE

AFTERWALE

BRIDLE AND
NECK COLLAR

HEAD PIECE

BROW BAND
ROSETTE

THROAT LATCH

CHEEK PIECE

BEARING REIN

TERRET

HAME TUG

TRACE

HAME

KIDNEY LINK

Pony harness, on the other hand, is also available over the counter—at a cost only slightly, if any, less than full-sized.

A Word of Caution

We have seen some Amish harness which just won't do. Beware of buckles stamped rather than cast. Be sure the driving reins are not too wide for your hands. The very cheapest line in some shops cuts too many corners to be practical or useful: the saving, in this case, is not worth it.

HARNESS—PIECE BY PIECE

Although harness requirements may vary a bit depending on the animal to be driven and the use it's to be put to, there are certain basic pieces common to all. The following on these essential parts will help the beginner understand each part's function and know better what to look for when purchasing them. A look at the accompanying diagrams will help too.

The Check Rein

The standard Amish harness comes with an overcheck, a strap and headpiece which runs from the bit over the head between the ears and then over the top of the neck to a hook fastened in the middle of the saddle. However, most pleasure drivers prefer side-check reins. These also attach

15. Check reins. As indicated on page 47, although the overhead check rein gives greater control and keeps the horse's head up, it is *not* recommended for pleasure driving.

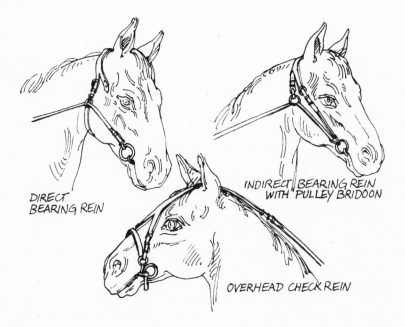

DIRECT
BEARING REIN

INDIRECT BEARING REIN
WITH PULLEY BRIDOON

OVERHEAD CHECK REIN

to the top of the bit, but then run on either side of the head
to loops connected to the crown piece of the bridle, hanging
well down toward the throat, and then to the check hook on
the saddle.

Harness-racing trainers and some of the breed associations use the overcheck, mainly to position the animal's
head where the trainer wants it: pleasure-driving people
feel that the overcheck works against the roof of the mouth
and that the side reins allow the horse to flex his neck comfortably while traveling on the road or cross-country, while
still preventing the head from getting down too low. But, in
the more sophisticated pleasure-driving turnouts, overchecks are not considered proper.

Bits

The standard driving bit supplied in an Amish harness is a
plain broken snaffle. This is perfectly all right for the beginner and for ordinary driving purposes. However, many
driving people prefer to use a Liverpool bit for single
horses. This has a straight bar in the horse's mouth, or
perhaps a bar with a moderate port (the arch in the
mouthpiece of the bit into which the tongue fits), and a curb
chain. As the bit diagram shows, the ordinary Liverpool offers the advantage of being able to adjust the bitting in your
horse's mouth to varying degrees of severity. The least severe setting on the Liverpool is less severe than the broken
snaffle. This is known as "smooth cheek," and rarely brings
the curb chain into action. The next setting, "rough cheek,"
exerts mild pressure on the mouth through the curb chain.
A third setting, "half cheek," provides additional leverage.
The fourth setting, "full cheek," should be used only in extreme cases of hard-mouthed or unruly horses requiring
extra leverage. This "full cheek," setting is sometimes re-
ferred to as the "dead man's hole"—an accurate, if somewhat wry, description.

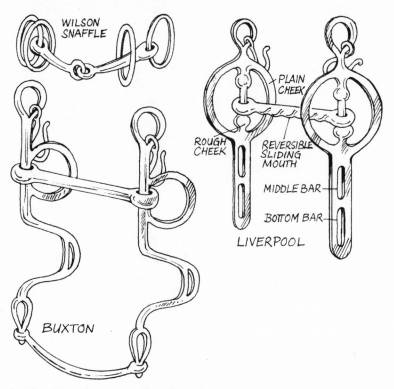

16. Bits. The Liverpool offers four degrees of (increasing) severity, depending on (respectively) whether the reins are attached to the rings, to the center branch below the mouthpiece, or to one of the two bar positions. The Buxton has three rein settings and is used with formal turnouts, particularly with pairs or fours-in-hand; its bottom crossbar prevents entanglement of the bit in the harness of another horse. Both the Buxton and the Liverpool may have sliding mouthpieces and fixed or swivel cheeks. The Wilson snaffle can provide three rein positions (starting with least severe): around both rings; around the outer rings on one side and both rings on the other; or around the outer rings only.

The Bridle

Amish bridles, with their standard overchecks leading to a simulated "figure eight" headpiece attached to the bit, do not include the nose strap (or cavesson, as more commonly known on a riding bridle) shown on the accompanying driv-

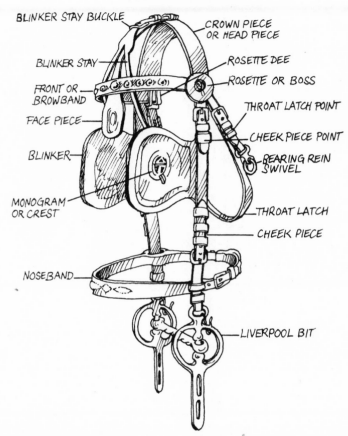

BLINKER STAY BUCKLE

CROWN PIECE
OR HEAD PIECE

BLINKER STAY

ROSETTE DEE

ROSETTE OR BOSS

FRONT OR
BROWBAND

THROAT LATCH POINT

FACE PIECE

CHEEK PIECE POINT

BLINKER

BEARING REIN
SWIVEL

MONOGRAM
OR CREST

THROAT LATCH

CHEEK PIECE

NOSEBAND

LIVERPOOL BIT

17. The driving bridle. More complicated than the riding bridle (since all control of the horse must come through the reins and the whip), the driving bridle has accommodations for bearing reins and for blinders, as seen here. This particular bridle features a Liverpool bit and the hatchet-shaped blinders.

ing bridle diagram. Again, most pleasure-driving trainers feel that such a strap, herein called a "noseband," provides more control of the horse. A simple black strap, 18 inches or so long, will do very nicely if it is buckled snugly to prevent the horse from opening his mouth when he feels pressure from the bit.

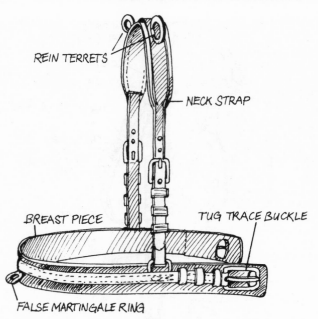

REIN TERRETS

NECK STRAP

BREAST PIECE

TUG TRACE BUCKLE

FALSE MARTINGALE RING

18. (*Above and opposite*). Details of the breast collar, and as used in single harness.

Generally speaking, the driving bridle is fitted a little tighter than the riding bridle. Again, this is for safety's sake. The throat latch should be kept as snug as possible without choking the horse. The nose strap should also be snug. The reason for this snugness: consider the danger threatened by a harnessed horse rubbing off his bridle against the point of a shaft or pole! Disaster would be imminent: the best the driver could do would be to unload fast and try for the horse's head. The ridden horse has nothing about him to rub on in the same way, unless his rider is so unwary as to go to sleep in the shade of a tree. Care should also be taken to have the cheek straps tight enough, holding the bit up against the bars of the horse's mouth on the one hand but not allowing the blinders to be pulled away from the sides

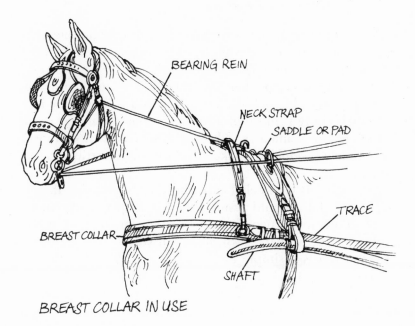

BEARING REIN

NECK STRAP

SADDLE OR PAD

TRACE

BREAST COLLAR

SHAFT

BREAST COLLAR IN USE

of the face on the other. A glimpse of the carriage behind him, hitherto hidden by the blinders, has been known to frighten more than one driven horse ordinarily believed to be a model of manners.

The Breast Collar—or Round?

The drawing above shows the breast collar, which, because it is looser-fitting than the round collar, can be used successfully by a number of similarly-sized horses. Beginners favor it for this reason. The round collar (shown, for example, in Figures 14, 19, 20 and 22, among others) requires a rather close fit for each horse, often involving a number of collars for a more-than-one- or two-horse barn.

The Girth and Tie-down

Some Pennsylvania harness makers include a double girth with connections to the tugs (leather loops) through which the shafts pass. These connections are designed to keep the shafts from rising up when the horse is working against the breeching to hold back the carriage. In a four-wheeled vehicle such rising is more of a nuisance than a danger, so the Amish harness makers, whose home clients use mostly four-wheeled vehicles, make the restraining straps rather loose.

But, with a two-wheeled cart, there is much more danger that rising shafts could result in the cart tipping over backwards. Thus many people augment the double girth with a tie-down strap which attaches to both shafts, passing under the horse. It is a simple device with a buckle at each end. We recommend it highly from the point of view of safety. Also, with some of the more elegant carts, the breeching is discarded and is replaced by brass straps on the shafts at the shaft tugs. These work to hold back the forward motion of the vehicle. With this arrangement the tie-down strap provides a double safety factor.

The Martingale

Another piece of harness you might want is the martingale. Martingales are sometimes used if the horse's head's carriage is too high. They are available in the Amish harness stores and are used on the Amish horses, as well as on many horses driven in the breed show rings. However, most pleasure driving people feel that the martingale is no substitute for proper training and should be dispensed with as soon as possible. Now and then one sees a *false* martingale used with a breast collar, but they are more familiar with the heavier type of harness using a round collar. These do little except to keep the collar from riding up too high on the chest and are mainly for decoration—certainly, they are not a necessary part of the light single-horse driving harness.

For Greater Elegance

Later on, if your enjoyment of driving leads you toward competition or just to more elegance, it will be best to have your harness made by one of a number of qualified harness makers now working in the United States and Canada. The difference between an Amish harness and one made specifically for your horse is much the same as a man buying a suit off the rack in a discount store versus having one custom made.

Any upgrading of harness from the simpler harness described in this chapter becomes considerably more expensive. As the beginning driver becomes more expert and ventures farther afield from his home barn and buys one of the more elegant vehicles discussed in the earlier chapters, his harness must be upgraded as well. Brass fittings, coaching-style bridles and collars, perhaps a gig pad and French-style shaft tugs—all these and more—become part of the "necessaries," and they all cost considerably more than the basic single harness. As we saw, the basic Amish harness in the late 1970's ranged in the neighborhood of $130; makers of fine harness at this same time were asking $1,500 or better for a single show harness. It is futile to ask fine craftsmen to make a cheap harness; not only do they not want to be associated with inexpensive and ordinary work, they can make far more money filling orders for more elegant harness. The major virtues of the simpler Amish harness—besides its low price tag—are its strength and safety.

THE HARNESSING ROUTINE

At Kellington Farm we believe in following a series of routine moves in placing the harness on any horse and then in placing the horse in the carriage. We emphasize this. Our rule is: establish a routine and then stick to it as in the old Army way of doing it "by the numbers." It may seem unnecessarily monotonous, but it helps to avoid that most dangerous factor in driving—forgetting to fasten every needed strap and buckle.

As we review the harnessing routine together, frequent reference to the harness drawings on pages 44, 45 and 51 should prove helpful, as will close study of the photographs—some of which we have been graciously permitted to reprint here in "Harnessing with the Round Collar" (pages 56–59)—that Philip Hofmann prepared for *Practical Horseman* magazine. Note the slight differences in harnessing sequence between the use of the breast collar and the round collar.

"Dressing" the Horse

1. *First the saddle-crupper.* As to the proper order, it makes little difference whether a *breast* collar is put on over the horse's head before or after the saddle-crupper-backstrap combination—though when putting on a *round* collar that must be the first thing because the breast plate must be fastened to the girth. The important thing is that it be done the same way each time.

However, we prefer to work from back to front. This means that we put the saddle-crupper-backstrap on first. The harness saddle should sit behind the withers by several inches—in the middle of the area which would be covered by a riding saddle. It is held in that position by the girth, and by the backstrap which attaches to the crupper under the horse's tail. The girth must always be taken up slowly for there is just as much chance of a "cold-backed" (sensitive) horse resenting the abrupt tightening of the harness girth as there is when saddling a riding horse. The safety strap, or belly band, can be left loosely attached at this point. The backstrap should be taut and the crupper should be snug against the root of the tail. Nothing looks worse than a crupper dangling below the root of the tail or a loose backstrap bouncing up and down on the horse's spine.

Caution is taken when placing the crupper under the tail to make sure that none of the tail hairs are caught in it: this to avoid any irritation or soring of the under part of the tail. A helpful hint: if getting the tail through the crupper opening proves difficult, the tail can be neatly folded, pulled through and then straightened out when through.

2. *Next the breeching.* Once the saddle-crupper-backstrap combination is secure is the time to run the breeching straps through the backstrap: there is a specific slot for this. The breeching placement must be neither too high nor too low. The horizontal breeching strap should rest just where the rump curves into the leg. Have it too high and the breeching strap tends to ride up over the rump toward the root of the tail; have it too low and the weight of the carriage inhibits the freedom of action of the hind legs, and on some steep grades actually exerts a lifting pressure against the hindquarters.

3. *Next the breast collar.* The collar goes on with the traces (the heavy leather straps which run alongside the shafts and serve to attach the vehicle to the horse's collar) already in place. Its fit is very important: as the harnessing sequence shows, it should rest a finger or two below the very base of the neck, but in no case lower than the middle of the shoulder—any lower than that will interfere with the free movement of the forelegs which is so necessary. As we said earlier, if we were using a round collar, the order would be reversed, with the collar going on first and then the saddle-crupper combination.

4. *Next the bridle and reins.* Our next step is to run the driving reins through the saddle terrets, letting the bit ends

(Continued on page 59*)*

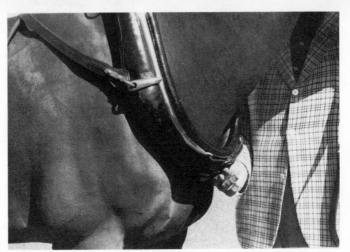

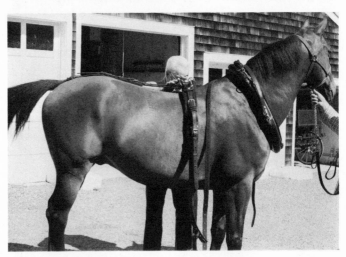

STEP 1

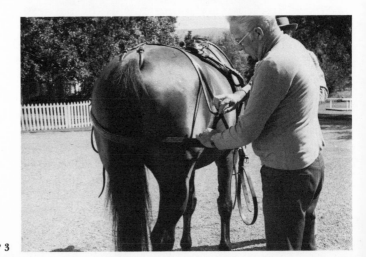

STEP 2

STEP 3

19. **Step 1 (opposite top):** The collar is put on with the traces already attached and placed over the horse's head upside down; this allows the head more room. Once on, the collar is turned and the traces temporarily crossed over the horse's neck so they won't be stepped on during the harnessing. A proper fitting collar is important: it should be close-fitting without rubbing and, as in Figure 19, show little or no daylight between the neck and collar. The technique for harnessing with a breast collar can be different (see the text for the author's preference).

20. **Step 2 (opposite center):** Next the saddle is placed on the horse's back, though not tightened until the tail is run through the crupper (here again, see text for more detail). Once the crupper is on, the saddle is lifted forward until it sits neatly behind the horse's withers; the photo shows the position. Next the saddle is firmly fixed by tightening the girth and safety strap. The girth should be taken up slowly; some horses resent a girth and will try to bloat up so that the girth will not fit snugly. The safety strap should always fit loosely, with about two fingers of space between it and the girth; otherwise, the horse will be pinched between.

21. **Step 3 (opposite bottom):** Next the breeching strap is run over the horse's back through the backstrap and fastened, making sure that the horizontal strap will be approximately even with the shafts' final position. The breeching strap is fastened on the off side of the horse.

22. **Step 4 (below):** Next, go to the head and slip off the horse's halter, taking care to run it around his neck so he can't slip away. The bridle is then put on and the throatlatch fastened loosely. Then the noseband is fastened: a common mistake is to have the noseband too loose; there should be only about two fingers space between the strap and the horse. This picture shows the bit just about to go into the horse's mouth. Once the bridle is secure, check once more to make sure everything is fastened as it should be and give the girth a final check. When all is secure, bring up the cart—or carriage.

(Continued)

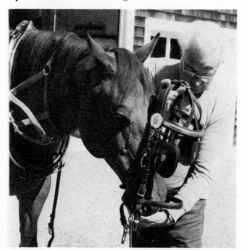

STEP 4

STEP 5

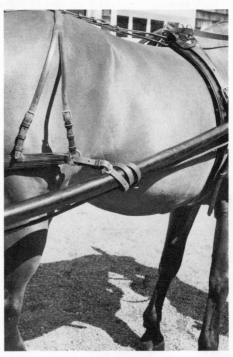

STEP 6

23. **Step 5 (opposite top):** Always bring the cart to the horse, especially when either the owner/driver or the horse is green. And always try to have two people available at this stage: there is too much opportunity for trouble otherwise. As the cart is brought forward around the horse, run the shafts through the tugs (loops) on either side of the backstrap. This photo shows the cart at just about this stage.

24. **Step 6 (opposite bottom):** Next, uncross the traces from around the horse's neck and run one back on one side and hook it to that side of the cart. Immediately after, go to the other side (or make sure your helper is doing it) and run back the opposite trace. It is essential that these both be fastened; thus, should the horse move off, he would have both sides of the vehicle secured to him. Once the traces are fastened down, the breeching is further secured. It is run through a dee-ring on the shaft, wrapped around the shaft three times and then buckled to itself, as shown here. Note that the breeching encircles the traces as well, thereby securing them to the shafts.

---

hang loose but not low enough to be stepped on; the hand ends are looped around the backstrap using a slip knot which can be pulled free instantly, when/if needed. Next the bridle goes on (you'll see that clearly in Step 4 of the accompanying photo sequence), then the bit ends of the reins are attached to the bit in the proper setting of severity (this, of course, for our Liverpool; your bit might or might not have a degree of severity as we saw in the bit section). Then the throat latch, noseband and curb are fastened and the position of the blinkers checked.

5. *A final check.* When the work at the front end is finished, we return to the mid-section to recheck the girth and to make sure it is pulled up to its regular snugness. Usually by now the horse knows you mean business and this will be no problem.

Adding the Vehicle

Once the horse is properly "dressed" in his harness he can be led to the vehicle, or the vehicle brought to him. Some of us can remember the family driving horse of grandfather's day which would back up into a carriage or wagon's shafts on command while the driver held the reins in one hand and the shafts at the proper height with the other. This might have been necessary on the farm when dealing with a loaded wagon, and there is no reason why such a stunt cannot be taught today, but it is a frill which is no longer important *if* the training of the horse to stand where he is put has been thorough and the lesson well learned. We feel it is much better to bring the cart to the horse. Most breaking carts, jog carts and/or carriages we've recommended for the beginning driver are light enough to be pulled forward to the horse with very little effort.

1. *Bringing up the vehicle.* Working from the near (left) side of the horse, the vehicle is moved gently toward the horse with the shafts held slightly above the back. Care should be taken not to let the shafts run against the horse or catch in the harness, and it is very important that the vehicle not bump the horse's hindquarters as it is pulled forward. A level place in the yard is the best location for this operation.

2. *Attaching the vehicle.* As the vehicle comes to the horse the driver (the beginner may want a helper at first) should guide the shafts through the tugs on the near side. The driver then moves to the off (other) side and repeats the operation, after which he unwraps the traces and attaches them to the vehicle on both sides.

Next come the straps which connect the breeching to the shafts. A double wrap is preferable: this is done by passing the strap first through the "dee," or fitting, on the under side of the shaft; then, after taking two turns encircling both the shaft and the trace, passing the tongue of the breeching strap under the first wrap before it is buckled.

It is important that the traces and breeching are adjusted one to the other so that slack in either will be avoided. The trick here is to have the traces taut when attaching the breeching straps to the shafts. We like at least three fingers between the horse's rump and the breeching. Any more and there is a certain amount of forward and backward jerking which is hard on the whip and any passengers—and even harder on the horse.

Lastly, the bellyband is buckled, the tie-down likewise, and the checkrein connected to the saddle hook.

Practice Makes Perfect

With the checkrein done up you are ready to pull the driving reins free of their slip knot, get into your vehicle and move out. But we suggest you stay. We suggest you then reverse the entire procedure all the way back to the horse standing stripped except for his halter. Then run through the entire harnessing procedure again, right up to the moment of mounting into the carriage.

The more times you fully dress your horse and put him in the cart, the more firmly you establish the routine and the safer a driver you will become. One strap carelessly left unbuckled can cause a serious accident, and possibly a runaway horse. You might liken yourself to an airplane pilot with a check list to run down before taking off. The old-time coachman, whether he harnessed the team himself or had it done by grooms, never mounted the box without running through a mental check list, walking from horse to horse and from side to side to make certain everything was in order. Four horses or one, the same care makes for safe, happy driving for pleasure.

In studying and working on these harnessing steps it is

25. William Radebaugh uses the coaching horn to call the 1977 Lake Mohonk Drive. Among those anxious to get going, behind this fine Hackney pair, are Clement Hoopes and his wife, Ellie.

easy to see the virtues of a horse that can be depended upon to stand where he is put; otherwise it would be impossible to work alone and much less than pleasant even with help. The well-trained horse permits the handler to move from one side to another as often as necessary to harness him. If the horse won't stand still during this operation someone will be needed to hold him. At the first sign of a horse that won't stand still resolve right then and there to return the horse to his preliminary training until he stands like a rock.

CARE OF EQUIPMENT

Constant attention to the condition and care of both vehicle and harness is essential to continued driving pleasure.

The Vehicle

All moving vehicles require lubrication, for both ease of operation and proper preservation. Even the modern jog carts require frequent lubrication of their wheels as an important maintenance procedure. Proper tightness of the hub nuts is also vital: nothing is more upsetting to horse *and* driver than to suddenly lose a wheel. With proper care, this shouldn't happen. Wheels should be watched constantly for loose spokes and worn tires, both rubber and steel. If you drive a four-wheeled vehicle, the king bolt which connects the front axle to the body of the carriage should be inspected frequently to make certain it is secure.

Antique carriages should be watched for signs of age—both dry rot and metal fatigue. To guard against metal fatigue be sure that both the running gear and cast iron parts of the shafts and undercarriage get frequent inspection. However, most older carriages were built to last for decades—built-in obsolescence was not popular then—so chances are that, if they have been cared for over the years, most antique vehicles may well be as strong as they were when built.

The Harness

Cleaning harness, particularly the Amish makes, is as important for safety as it is for appearance. At Kellington Farm we start with a wash using Castile soap and a sponge barely dampened in warm water, rather than washing with saddle soap which we find too greasy. The Castile soap cuts through the old dirt and grease on the harness much as a detergent does, and leaves the surface extra clean. We then dry the harness with turkish-type toweling. Following that, liquid glycerine—we prefer Bentley—is rubbed into the leather to restore the natural oils.

We do not use saddle soap on any harness which we might want to polish since the saddle soap prevents a shine. Boot polish—black for black harness and tan for russet—is used on all but everyday exercising harness, and liquid glycerine or saddle soap rubbed on the undersides of all straps and collars as a softener and preservative. We usually use Kiwi or Mennonite Creme boot polishes.

All buckles must be undone and the leather under them cleaned and carefully treated since these are the areas most vulnerable to wear and rot; also, wherever the leather is curved, or folded, passing around metal rings, buckles, etc., it should receive special attention.

Nickel hardware can be washed off or rubbed off; brass fittings can be cleaned and shined with a metal polish—we like Brasso—care being taken not to let any metal polish get on the leather.

Shoeing

The driving horse's equipment—his shoes—also need care. In fact, the driving horse requires more attention to his shoeing than does the hunter or hack. Whereas the ridden horse travels very little, if at all, on hard roads, the driving horse gets a great deal of mileage on hard roads. Even gravel roads cause as much wear on shoes as do roads of macadam and concrete. As a result the ridden horse is far less apt to wear out his shoes before the growth of his hoofs dictates reshoeing; the driven horse, on the other hand, often does. During the driving season, Kellington Farm horses are shod every five weeks, if not more often. Leather pads are always worn on the front feet except during the non-working periods. The heel caulk used depends on the individual horse.

Whether or not to use borium on the hoofs of driving horses during the summer is open to debate. Some whips point to the slipperiness of macadam or concrete as justification for borium; however, some veterinarians and farriers insist that the "grabbing" action of the rough metal on hard roads leads to leg strain and injury. Undoubtedly borium performs a valuable secondary function in that it adds to the life of the shoe. Each whip will have to decide for himself whether the possible danger is worth it.

No one chapter could cover the whole world of harness, its uses and management. For more information, look to several good sources in the bibliography. A trip to one of the leading harness makers is another way to learn—and of course collections of harness as well as antique carriages are found at the leading carriage museums. However, it is our hope that the harnessing information given here will give you enough background and how-to to get you safely and not too expensively on the road.

5

Training

N O W—your horse and vehicle selected, your harness chosen and carefully applied—you're ready to drive. Let's assume that the horse you plan to drive has been ridden, or at least has had some rudimentary training and handling—that he or she has been broken to halter and to lead quietly, to stand where put, to accept a bit and girth and to obey the command "whoa." Ideally, he has also been longed successfully both ways of the ring. These, as any horseman knows, are the first steps in the training of any young horse—whether for saddle or for harness.

Generations of experienced horsemen have believed that training in harness is the best way to start *any* young horse regardless of what the animal's ultimate destiny. With the exception of those working with Thoroughbred racing stock, trainers of almost all other breeds—in America as well as abroad—follow this practice. They point to the fact that a young horse can be worked in harness at far less danger to his immature back and legs than when ridden. It is not unusual to find young two-year-old stock between the shafts of light breaking or jogging carts. This allows development of the muscular structure as well as the heart and lungs, and at the same time teaches early submission to the lessons of discipline the young horse must accept throughout its working life whether going under saddle, over jumps or in harness.

WHEN TO START

Off the race tracks most trainers defer ridden exercise until late in the two-year-old span, but many are willing to schedule light driven work by the same animal on a regular basis somewhat earlier. Much depends on the individual colt or filly; obviously a late spring or summer foal would not have progressed as far in the summer of its two-year-old year as one born several months earlier, and no two foals mature in identical fashion.

Many two-year-olds are seen in the breed show rings in harness. Almost without exception, however, they are not asked to do anything more strenuous than walk and trot around a smooth, level ring—whether in training or in competition. They are given little, if any, road work, and most of them don't begin to see the open spaces beyond the ring until well along in their three-year-old year.

In the world of driving for pleasure on the road, and in the many driving and carriage competitions, even three-year-olds are more rare than usual. Here, again, much depends on the individual animal—both physically and temperamentally. For instance, much work and training is done at this stage with the draft breeds which seem to mature earlier in all respects. Many of the crossbreds seen in driving sport these days seem to reflect the rather phlegmatic temperament of their draft-horse blood, many also inheriting the bone and muscle of their draft-horse dams while retaining the spirit, brightness and much of the body conformation of their Thoroughbred, Standardbred or Hackney sires. Such young can be worked safely as two-year-olds.

At Kellington Farm we once purchased a pair of Hackney–French Coach crossbred. This was in July, and having been told they were mid-summer foals we assumed they were already 36 months old. This particular pair had been bred and broken to harness in the Lake Huron area of Ontario, Canada. There they had been driven to a manure spreader from January on, and had been shown in the small local competitions for commercial-type horses in the area. When they arrived at Kellington Farm they were fat and had the outsized hooves favored by the Canadian farmers of their native region. They went right into training at our place and were shown in carriage competitions through October of that year before being rested for several months— all this without our realizing that they were not yet three. They continued to mature slowly but never showed any ill effects from that work. We have always been thankful that this breakdown in communication didn't do any damage. Not all horses could have been treated that ruggedly without harm.

Perhaps a good guide when deciding when to start working a horse in harness is to remember that the most grueling tests of a driving horse's stamina, working under organized rules, are those in the cross-country phase of FEI combined driving competitions. Under these rules a horse is asked to go up to 26 miles at an average speed of about 8 miles an hour. Until 1976, the FEI mandated that horses must be at least five years old to compete, but that year the international body reset the age limit at four. Thus it is to be assumed that a four-year-old is up to anything in harness competition, and anything comparable outside competition.

TRAINING STEPS

Training the older horse to accept harness and carriage is a great deal easier if he has been driven as a colt. However, since many riding horse owners have no knowledge of their animal's early experiences, in most instances the trainer or owner/trainer must begin driving instruction slowly and proceed step by step as he would with a green horse—that is, once the basic obediences (to lead quietly, to stand, to accept the bit and girth and to obey "whoa") have been attained. If these basics haven't yet been mastered, that must be accomplished before driving training can begin.

Settling In

When a horse comes to Kellington Farm to be trained in harness our initial procedure is to do as little as possible with him for the first 48 hours. We give the new member that time to adjust to his new stall, the sounds of the new stable, the voices of the new people around him, and the feeding and other routines. He may be turned out in a roomy pen where he can watch the other horses—even touch noses—for some of his first hours in his new residence. Of course, in many cases, the horse to be trained will already be "at home," and this adjustment won't be necessary.

The Bitting Harness

The first actual step in training the horse to drive is to introduce him to the bitting harness. This is best done while he is still in his stall.

The bitting harness consists of a broad combination saddle and girth with both reins and a back strap leading to a crupper and can be bought in most shops which sell horse equipment. In earlier days, they were often made of leather but today most of them are made of strong webbing and felt with an open bridle. This simple harness is an invaluable aid in training the horse to carry his head properly, respond to light pressures from a bit, and to learn the feeling of harness on his body.

26. (*Above*). A bitting harness in use with long lines, which are fastened to the bit and run through terrets on the back pad.

27. (*Below*). Exercise on the longe teaches maneuverability and discipline.

The bitting harness should be put on loosely at first, with the girth barely snug and both the bearing and check reins allowing plenty of slack. Gradually—over a period of several days to a week, as the training progresses—the reins are shortened and the girth tightened a hole at a time until the horse is under firm control.

The bit should be nothing more severe than a bar snaffle or a "mouthing" bit, unless you are working with a fully mature animal which is already familiar with bitting pressures. Later a driving Liverpool may be substituted.

The bitting harness should not be left on the horse, regardless of his experience and age, for more than a short period—perhaps up to a half hour—but may be put on in the morning and again in the afternoon.

Longeing

Once the horse has had several hours of this in his stall, the horse should be taken out—to a ring if one is available—and longed while wearing the bitting harness, the reins used to hold his head in the driving position, slightly flexed at the poll.

It is more than likely that some tension will be evidenced at first. The reins and checkreins constitute a new form of discipline to the riding horse and most of them will show some objection. And of course green stock is also apt to resist at first. To deal with this, longeing should continue firmly but quietly until the horse accepts the restraints on his head and neck movements, and the tension within the animal disappears. This should come fairly quickly in the case of the seasoned riding horse, while the two-year-old may take a little longer to relax and go forward smoothly. Again, the temperament of the individual horse has a significant bearing on the length of this portion of the training.

Short training periods are always best. Each time you achieve the results you are working toward it is time to think of ending that particular session. The time can lengthen as the training goes on but a half hour is likely the maximum at first, with an hour about the longest at any time. And when working on one step, don't push on to the next step until you are sure your pupil has the first one firmly in mind.

Driving in Long Lines

Driving in long lines is the next step, and perhaps one of the most important. Many amateurs consider long-lining just another form of longeing, but it isn't: it begins the teaching of response to the reins which longeing does not. Here the learning horse discovers the feel of human hands on his mouth, as transmitted through the reins and bit, and begins to recognize the signals for forward movement imparted by a light touch of the whip and the driver's voice rather than through a rider's legs or heels.

Long lines can be made by joining together leather reins, webbing, even fabric clothesline—with light snaps tied into the bit ends. The lines should be long—up to 15 feet, or more—so that the trainer can stand well back and to one side as the horse moves pretty much in a circling pattern. They should be light, and very flexible—clothesline of plastic is no good here—and reasonably strong. The idea is not to exert any more pressure on the horse's mouth than is absolutely necessary. At the same time he must not be allowed to get free from control at any time and the trainer should remember that the horse will not differentiate between a broken rein and a dropped rein. The trainer should have a longeing whip—not for punishment but for signaling. (Instructions for handling the driving whip are in the "Working the Horse" section later in this chapter; the longeing whip is of course different, but some of the same signals can be employed.)

At the beginning of the long-line training stage, it is best—in fact, almost essential—to have at least one assistant at the horse's head. Two would be even better, one at each side. Each assistant holds a lead rope attached to his or her side of the halter which is kept on under the bridle. As the trainer asks the horse to move forward so do the assistants. Their job is to gently pull the horse's head in the direction sought by the trainer through the reins, or to restrain the horse from turning too sharply. It is not their job to pull the horse forward: that impulsion must come from behind through the trainer's voice and his use of light pressure from the reins being laid across the hind legs just above the hocks and with light touches from the whip.

As in the other training stages, each animal will progress differently. The assistants can be excused once the horse responds to guidance through the bit and turns evenly and willingly in either direction. A relaxed horse is the next goal—the aim being a horse that will walk along at ease with himself and his driver. Fretting, headtossing, jigging and jogging—these are problems that had best be ironed out at the beginning before the added complication of cart or carriage. The horse that goes steadily and quietly in long lines is ready for the next step, and the time taken getting him to that point is well worth it.

Some driver/trainers like to take advantage of the long-line stage of driving training to get the horse completely familiar with the feel of the reins. They do this at various points in the training by gently allowing the reins to run all over the horse's body: this so that the horse will not be startled later when/if a flapping rein might touch him where he was not expecting it. Obviously care must be taken not to confuse the learning horse when he is concentrating on his directional signals. In much the same way, many trainers go

to great pains to expose driving horses to many of the obstacles and noises they may encounter once they reach the
road stage.

Pulling Weight

Many horses have to be taught to pull weight. Pressure on
their shoulders frightens some. In rural New England a
century ago the accepted method was to hitch the horse to a
drag of some sort. This is still a good idea. But a lot of the
old-timers made one serious mistake: they made the drag
too heavy. They used a log out of the woods, or a stoneboat
and when the green horse first felt his shoulders held by
such a large and unaccustomed force from behind he would
become frightened, and would try to back away from the
pressure—often resulting in a war between horse and
trainer.

To meet this problem today, some trainers advocate quite
another technique—the use of an assistant working behind
the horse. The horse is still in long lines and bitting harness
with the collar and traces added. The assistant walks behind
the horse holding the ends of the traces lengthened as
necessary by ropes or straps and gradually leaning back
against the forward motion of the horse by pulling gently
on the traces. There is nothing wrong with this system except that it takes two people; also, unless the assistant is experienced, the pressure applied is often either too much,
too little or too uneven.

Our experience at Kellington Farm has convinced us that
use of a very light drag just heavy enough to keep the traces
from flopping around the horse's hind legs is the best system. To make our drag we took a five-foot length of gal-
vanized water pipe, tied to a single-tree (a bar sometimes
used to ease the pull from the traces to the vehicle) taken
from an old wagon. The horse in training first pulls the

drag around in the ring where the soft ground and grass muffles the rattle; after several such sessions the horse is then moved to the gravel and then to macadam. The gradual increase in noise from the soft surface to a harder one is a plus part of the training—in preparation for the sound of the carriage wheels which will be coming to the horse shortly.

Throughout these preliminary training steps—in long lines and pulling a drag—some secondary training is also going on. In the stable the horse is asked to lower his head when the collar and bridle are put on. Some horses object to the feeling of the crupper being placed beneath their tails; this is a good time to get them familiar with that. Frequent—gentle but firm—work at this stage will make harnessing that much easier, safer and quicker later on. During the work outside the horse is taught to stand for lengthy periods of time without fidgeting, to stop when asked, and to back on command (we'll have more on how to accomplish these commands as we go along). And, of course, he learns the feeling of a single harness on his body.

All of these lessons learned go toward the education of the well-mannered driving horse so important for happy driving!

Working with a Cart

Another popular method of working with horses came to fore when the old-time trainers felt the horse was ready to start work in cart or carriage: long poles of light wood were placed in the shaft tugs, and as the horse walked along, these poles were pushed against the horse's sides and shoulders to simulate the feeling of shafts. We don't feel this is necessary at Kellington, but doubt that it does any harm; indeed, it may help.

Bearing in mind the fact that unaccustomed weight is

frightening to a green horse, the horse's first vehicle should be as light as possible, although it must be strong. We have seen numerous so-called "breaking carts" made from discarded automobile parts, with heavy metal axles, wheels and sometimes even truck seats. These "Rube Goldberg" carts are then fitted out with long shafts. The result is a sturdy, but exceedingly heavy, apparatus with crushing weight on a horse's back and a turning radius much longer than necessary and even unsafe.

In contrast, as we have seen in the "Two-Wheeler" chapter, the best breaking cart is a simple vehicle of wood construction, with a standing platform for the driver behind a simple plank seat. The shafts need not be unduly long: if the horse is going to kick, he isn't ready for *any* cart. Wire-wheeled carts can be substituted for the wooden-wheeled variety, but the cart should fit the horse reasonably well—with the line of draft from the horse's shoulders to the cart's single-tree as horizontal to the ground as possible.

When first putting the horse into the cart, an assistant should be used. He should stand in front of the horse facing rear and holding the animal firmly at the head while the trainer attaches first the traces, then the breeching straps to the shafts and finally the tie-down, or safety, strap which passes beneath the horse's girth from shaft to shaft. The proper adjustment of the tie-down strap is also important to the comfort of the ride in a two-wheeled cart—too tight, and all the motions of the horse's body are felt in the driver's seat; too loose, and the vehicle sways like a boat in rough water. Trial and error is your best answer here. (For a quick refresher on these "putting to" steps, turn back to the photo spread and text in the last chapter.)

The position of the horse in the cart is very important. The tips of the shafts should come just to the point of the horse's shoulders or very slightly ahead, with the traces taut. Meanwhile the breeching should allow about two fingers of space between the horse and the holdback strap, with, as we said, the shafts as close to the horizontal as possible. Many novices hitch their horses too loosely. This results in a lot of play between collar and breeching which results in an uncomfortable ride with frequent jerky starts and stops. Not only is this uncomfortable, it can be unsafe: such jerks can break harness and single-trees suddenly. Fewer, but some, beginners go to the opposite extreme and bind their horses too tight. This can result in harness sores, galls and a forced shortening of gait.

One of the most common causes of driving accidents is the failure to attach all the necessary parts of the harness properly and securely. Each strap is important to the whole and it only takes one coming undone to nullify the effect of the entire harness. Leave one breeching strap undone and you've got no breeching action at all since any pressure will just twist the breeching around and off the horse's haunches. A trace which comes away from the single-tree can cause the horse to come out of the shafts altogether— with the result, in all probability, an accident.

We cannot overemphasize the importance of properly harnessing horse to cart. A case in point: a fox-hunting friend of long standing, but with little experience in driving, one day put his fail-safe hunter between the shafts of a cart but forgot to do up the breeching properly. The horse went very nicely until they hit a downgrade, the cart then running up on the horse's rump and hind legs. Frightened, the horse bolted. The driver then headed the horse into a stand of corn, another mistake as the sound of the full-grown stalks and ears of corn hitting the cart scared the horse even more. Happily, there were no physical injuries, but the cart was wrecked, the horse was made apprehensive, and the driver lost his budding zest for the sport of driving.

The smallest detail must not be overlooked. The little leather or rawhide thongs attached to the end of the single-tree are there to be pulled through holes drilled in the wood, thus holding the traces on the single-tree. Another case in point: one wintery afternoon in New York State, a novice driver starting out for a ride in a light cutter behind a well-trained hunting pony failed to pull the little leather safety device through and over the end of one trace. Inevitably the trace worked loose. Result: the pony pulled himself out of the shafts and the driver over the dashboard into the snow. The unsteerable sleigh was dragged sideways and overturned. Some breakage resulted and the pony became very apprehensive, as did the owner. A professional trainer had to be called in to restore confidences.

Once the green horse is properly harnessed in his breaking cart, you are almost ready to start working him. This we, at Kellington Farm, do in the ring with at least one assistant. But first, an additional safety factor is built in. The halter is left on the horse's head under the bridle and a longe line attached with the chain part crossing the horse's nose, off-side to near-side passing through the halter pieces (some trainers prefer to run a rope from the off-side bit ring over the horse's head and down through the near-side bit ring). Both methods are designed to control the horse in the event of disobedience and/or over-excitement, and to prevent a runaway, but have nothing to do with the actual driving of the horse.

The same technique used at the start of the long-lining phase of the training should be followed at the start of the actual driving phase: assistants should walk alongside, one at each side of the horse, chiefly to steady the animal if need be. However, they do have one additional function in this phase: to help the horse adjust to the pressure of the shafts. As the horse turns in answer to the bit he meets the resistance of one shaft on one shoulder or side and often the pressure of the other shaft on the opposite hip. Quite often the green horse will shrink away from this pressure. In this

28. Working the green horse. The more traditional breaking cart allows the driver to step on and off the cart from behind with greater ease.

case, the assistant on the outside of the circle pushes the shafts in the direction of the turn thus helping to reassure the horse that the difficulty isn't anything to worry him. Meanwhile, the other assistant exerts pressure in his direction with his lead line, but not with the safety line which is held loosely and never used except at the trainer's command.

Should you be working with an exceptionally skittish horse one way to help familiarize him with the cart is to *hold* it up by him when he is first asked to pull—rather than tying it. In that way the assistants can drop the cart and let him run out of it if he gets frightened. After a few tries he should become less fearful and ready to be tied in and to get down to work.

During the initial circles the trainer walks behind or to one side of the cart. Once the horse settles down to the new experience the trainer hops up on the cart platform and then sits on the seat, either astride or somewhat backwards, ready to step off onto the ground again should trouble start. During all this the trainer must be careful that his movements do not affect the pressure on the reins, and through them, the bit and the horse's mouth. For the non-professional, this takes a bit of practice.

Moving Out

Before the training can go any further, it is necessary to know how to execute the basic maneuvers. Close attention to these basics—and a lot of practice—should do it.

USING THE WHIP

This seems a good spot to say something about the proper use of the driving whip. It is astonishing that so many drivers do not understand the purpose of the whip. Whereas the horseback rider has legs and heels and shifts of weight as aids in signaling his mount, the driver must depend on voice commands and his whip. The use of the whip to flog the horse forward is a mark of poor reinsmanship, and almost as much of a no-no as slapping him on the rump with the reins to start him off or increase his speed. The latter habit results in a bad jerk on the horse's mouth and confusion in the properly trained animal's mind—a sure way to undermine good training. The driver who does not have the know-how to use his whip to full advantage as an aid is denying himself a valuable tool in the handling and enjoyment of his horse.

Different drivers will have their own preferences in whip handling, as in other things, but as a general rule, the whip is held lightly, but firmly, in the right hand at about a 45-degree angle across the body—the balance point pretty

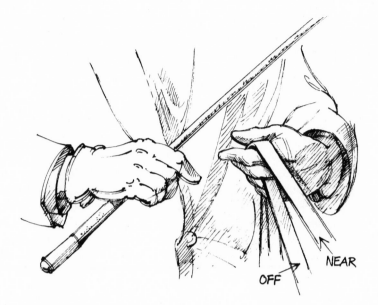

29. Holding the reins and whip for single horse driving.

much resting on the lower portion of the thumb (see illustration).

The whip is best applied between the collar and the pad, never on the hindquarters. To use the whip in helping to direct the horse: for a right turn, the whip is held horizontally to the right with the thong swung counter-clockwise; for a left turn, the whip is held to the left with the thong swung clockwise. To signal a stop, the whip is held upright over the center of the body.

HOLDING THE REINS

Each whip will perhaps develop his own pet way of holding and handling the reins, but the accepted way—when once seated properly—is to hold both reins in the left hand, with the near rein held over the index finger and the off rein held under the middle finger; the thumb points to the right, with the forefinger pointing slightly to the right rear (see illustration). The body should be straight and square with the elbows close to the side and the hands two to four inches in front of the body.

To Move Forward

First tighten the reins just enough to get the horse's attention; then give the command "walk on" in a firm voice. If he does not respond, repeat the command, at the same time touching him lightly on the shoulder with the whip. This should be sufficient. Then gradually ease up on the rein pressure as the horse moves forward.

Changing Direction

A left turn is executed by rotating the back of the rein (left) hand toward the body exerting pressure on the near rein and easing that on the off rein; this pressure can be increased, if necessary, by moving the hand slightly toward the right at the same time.

To make a right turn, the back of the hand is rotated away from the body; this increases pressure on the off rein and eases that on the near rein. To increase the pressure in this case, the rein hand moves slightly to the left while rotated. However, it is always preferable to keep the hands as close to the center of the body as possible.

To Stop

First give a firm "whoa" command and be prepared to shorten both reins equally using the right hand in front of the left and then sliding the left hand up behind the right to free that hand to do the same again if necessary. However, once should be sufficient. To slow the horse, use the same motion, but less firmly.

The Back-up

Backing should be taught fairly late in a horse's training. To teach backing the trainer or an assistant stand facing the horse: at the command to "get back," he or she pushes the horse's nose gently back with one hand and the chest with the other. If the horse doesn't respond after a few tries, the "front man" can tread lightly on one of the horse's hooves. As soon as the horse responds, he should be rewarded and led forward again. This routine is repeated over a period of time until the horse can be depended on to back three or four steps at a time without hesitation: he will quickly learn to do this at command, with just light pressure of the rein.

Back to the Practice Ring

Now that these basics are firmly in mind, it's back to the practice ring—and to more work by trainer, his assistants and the student horse. However, a little of this training routine goes a long way. It's wise not to extend these early lessons too long; maybe one or two hours at a time to begin with, but don't forget that putting the horse in and out of the cart several times during each lesson is good experience for both the green animal and for the novice driver. Once the horse gets used to his harness and his commands it is just a matter of time and mutual experience and understanding between horse and driver before a new driving team is born.

On the Road

On the open road, or cross-country, the horse must refine his normal instinct for balance in harness, even as the ridden horse must learn to carry weight up hill or down, and the hunter to carry a rider over fences safely. In addition the horse must accustom himself to the strangeness of it all.

Driving horses are frightened by the same things which scare them while being ridden. Some horses "spook" at one thing; some at others. The rattle of steel tires on pavement is a sound that ridden horses don't know and a sound that drivers should understand might upset a riding horse newly-trained to drive. One way to settle down a skittish newcomer might be to drive him for a while behind a seasoned horse so he can get used to the idea and strange sounds with confidence.

And in another vein, the budding driver must always recognize the limitations of space when sitting in cart or carriage. A saddle-horse—when met by a noisy truck—can sidle off the right of way; the harnessed horse cannot do that without danger to carriage and occupants. Drivers must be aware of dangers ahead at all times: here again, a great deal depends on the temperament of the individual horse.

Taking the Hills

Hills can be a problem. The weight of a carriage going downhill against the breeching is something a driving horse must learn to handle—again, experience in quiet surroundings a little at a time is the best way to train him. Newly-driven horses often view an approaching hill or upgrade with misgivings; some will attempt to gallop or charge up the hill, some will go only so far, then stop in fear of the pressure on their shoulders. Providing the way is clear there is no harm in letting the young horse canter a little beginning an upgrade; he needs the confidence that will grow as he masters the grade. Once he gains that, he probably will cease to charge hills all by himself; if not, he can be checked by his driver. The horse that quits half way up the hill is more of a problem. He has to be reassured. Generally he can be "restarted" by leading him with encouragement: he may scramble and plunge a bit, which is all right if he keeps going. Gradual and short slopes are the answer for him— over a period of time he'll find out he can do it. *Please*—no beating with the whip! That will just upset him more and he will associate the pain with the hill, making things even worse. This is a situation where there is no blueprint beyond just working with the horse to build up his ability, his confidence and his obedience.

THE DRIVER

Always, the driver must be alert. Alertness, and patient understanding, are the cardinal rules for the budding driver.

There have been exceptions which only prove the rule. Back in this writer's childhood a neighboring family numbered various hard-working, fairly uneducated lumbering brothers who were known for their ability to drink up most of their profits. Their place was a shambles and they were pretty nearly so. Their horses were shaggy, generally ungroomed, but always well fed. The general opinion was that the brothers fed their horses better than they fed themselves as a reward for the hard work they did. Regardless, Saturday nights in that small western Massachusetts town saw the men of the family stagger out of their favored haunts, crawl into the back of a light wagon and pass out. One somehow always managed to untie the horse in the shafts before joining his brothers in alcoholic slumber. Through the city streets and over the country roads the old horse took his cargo of bodies home, often standing in the shafts until morning and the brothers came alive again.

At the same time, many of us who are longer in the tooth than we would like to admit can recall the milk wagon horse which pulled his cargo quietly along while the driver ran from door to door making his deliveries. That horse could round corners by himself and could even stop at intersections, but of course he never did learn to read traffic lights or to count to ten before proceeding through a stop sign.

These are true stories, but there are few of us, particularly in this age of fast cars and heavy traffic, who would like to trust any horse to make a five-mile trip from mid-city to country or to deliver the neighborhood's milk unguided by human hands on the reins. And we shouldn't!

No matter how well-trained your driving horse becomes, the latter years of the 20th century are no time for him to go on his own, no matter how quiet the countryside he is going through may be. Now, the horse, like the animals of the wild, has to be protected from the dangers of the motor age, rather than from hereditary enemies. Whether on highway or byway the alert driver must consider the way ahead and the threats it may hold for this treasured relic of the past—the horse and carriage. This is an integral part of training your horse to drive—training yourself to drive the horse!

6

Driving for Fun

LET US BEGIN with the following elements—a
well-trained horse in good condition, a surrey with or without the "fringe on top," a day when the weather just begs
for an outing, and a group of fellow yearners for the open
road (four is a good number—of any and all ages). These
elements, put together, call for a drive, and if you have a
favorite picnic spot high on a hill or by the pond down in
the valley, so much the better. What's ahead is a lot of driving just for fun.

A PICNIC DRIVE

First—Prepare!

While the picnic food is being fixed in the house there are
several definite chores to do in the barn. Check your harness to be certain it is safe and sound. Be sure your horse's
shoes are tight and not too worn, for nothing can spoil the
fun of a drive faster than a lost shoe miles from home. Pull
out the surrey (or whatever vehicle you have available to

use) and think back to when the wheels were greased last: the ordinary daily use of a vehicle does not require fresh greasing of its wheels each time you use it, but it is far safer to freshen the axles at the start of an all-day drive than to risk a dry or seized hub somewhere along the way. But most of all, look to your tool kit!

The Tool Kit

A tool kit is more important to a carriage than it is to the modern automobile. The basic items carried in that kit are there for the safety of horse and humans and the sensible driver will not leave his home ground without a fully stocked kit.

The Standards for Competitions of the American Driving Society (ADS) in the section devoted to timed marathons (2.11A) lists the contents of the tool kit which each vehicle must carry. Each item has a particular purpose and could be called into use along the way; if one is missing, a driver could be in serious trouble. This is just as true for a picnic drive as for a timed marathon. The list calls for the following: a leather punch, wheel wrench, jackknife, screwdriver, small hammer, a length of rawhide, string or wire, a rein splicer (or spare rein), a trace splicer (or a spare trace), a hame strap if your harness is one with a round collar, hoof pick, halter and lead shank, plus a cooler or blanket depending on the weather. If you look this list over carefully you'll see that there is a good use for each item. If this seems like an awful lot of gear to carry on a simple day's outing consider the alternative—perhaps a breakdown on the road or on a trail far from quick and experienced help.

Actually the gear required by the ADS rules, with the exception of the halter and cooler or blanket, can fit into a man's small traveling kit such as the kind he takes to hold toilet articles. (At Kellington Farm, we sometimes use the

30. A summer picnic drive seen from the seat of a roof-seat break; the photo showing a pair harness in lively action.

wooden artist boxes.) A spare trace can be coiled into a compact roll. A rein splicer is a simple piece of leather strap 6 to 12 inches long with a buckle at each end, and since reins seldom break we take the splicer rather than a spare rein. Major repairs are not the idea behind the tool kit, emergency ones are. A broken wheel is left for the wheelwright but a leather punch and a piece of cord can fix broken harness. Kellington Farm tool kits carry pliers or an adjustable wrench and a roll of black tape in addition to those items required under the ADS rules.

A Personal Experience

Almost anyone who has had much driving experience has a story to tell in regard to the need for a well-stocked tool kit.

We are no exception. Several years ago we were guests on a picnic drive in a remote section of the Berkshire Hills of western Massachusetts. The cavalcade of seven or eight vehicles left the road and traveled deep into the woods to reach a delightful spot by the side of a private pond where a picnic area had been set up. Horses were unhitched and tied in the shade for about two hours while the luncheon and wine were consumed, and as is the case quite often, the horses became restless. Our big veteran hunter and driving horse was no exception. By the time it came time to go back and for him to be put into the shafts, he was a handful, and despite the experience of his driver and passenger, he suddenly lunged forward, snapping a trace right up at the buckle on his round collar.

Some of the party had gone on ahead, but we were holding up others. It was not a life or death situation, but annoying to say the least and involving the possibility of a long walk back to the road where we could be met by a truck, a horse trailer—and rescue.

But we were lucky: help came sooner than we deserved in the form of one of the experienced drivers on the ride. From his tool kit he produced a length of strong nylon cord and quickly attached the broken trace to the buckle. We were soon on our way again—thanks to the contents of that well-stocked tool kit.

How Far to Go

How far you plan to go on any particular day's picnic drive depends on a number of things, such as how fit the horse is, how hilly and rough the route is, and how hot the day. Most fit carriage horses pulling a light surrey (or similar vehicle), even with four people in it, can manage a rate of seven miles an hour if the going isn't too steep. A drive of from five to eight miles each way is reasonable—more can be

31. John Jenkle of Sebastopol, California, driving his fine American Standardbreds to a roof-seat break at the American Driving Society's 1977 driving weekend at Lake Mohonk, New York.

traveled with pleasure if the route is level and the weather fresh.

Which Vehicle to Take

Some vehicles work better than others for a picnic drive. For instance, the surrey we spoke about above really has very little cargo space; thus if the food and drink are going to be carried on board, some one of the party is likely going to have to straddle the picnic hamper, be it wicker, cardboard or whatever. The horse's cooler or blanket can be sat on. If picnics are to be the single-carriage family's chief concern, obviously that should be a major consideration in their choice of vehicle, as we have discussed at length in the "Four-Wheelers" chapter. But that is seldom the case. Beyond that, the beginning driver often just has to make do

the best he can with what he has. Certainly a slightly
crowded picnic is better than no picnic at all!

LONG-DISTANCE DRIVES

Not all picnic drives have to be limited to a day's drive
across nearby terrain. Longer trips involving overnight stays
are great fun, though of course when the billeting and feeding of both horses and passengers must be arranged the
logistics can get quite complicated. Such drives can be
planned on a rather luxurious basis, with overnight stops
planned at inns or other such establishments along the way,
or on a more rugged basis. Overnight camping is certainly a
possibility, although this route may well require mechanical
back-up by way of a truck to act as supply train and
emergency resource.

The preparations for long-distance drives must, of
course, be even more arduous than those for the day's picnic, and such drives are not to be undertaken lightly—but
the satisfactions are enormous when the proper preparations are made and both horses and participants are fit
and eager.

A Vermont Drive

One especially fine long-distance drive comes immediately
to mind. In September of 1976 William Davisson of
Marlboro, Vermont drove a pair of Connemara mares put
to a park phaeton (much like a surrey) 70-odd miles from
his home in Marlboro to South Woodstock, another Vermont town. It was a leisurely trip of four days with the actual driving time on the road averaging about five hours
each day, with a rest stop and luncheon break of at least an
hour and a half at the halfway points. The longest single-
day mileage was 22.2 miles. Davisson had planned his trip

well in advance, his maps showing 48.2 miles on dirt roads and 25.6 on macadam. Much of the trip was done at the walk and much of it was hilly.

The mares handled the trip without incident as did a Hackney pony pulling a light road wagon. The weather was cool but not chilly. The rear seat of the phaeton was given over to gear for the three animals and a light trunk attached to the rear of the carriage held more equipment for the humans as well as the ponies.

This was no wagon train, nor was it a marathon drive. It was strictly driving for pleasure. Davisson wasn't trying to prove anything or set any records. He spent the nights in quiet country inns, he took his time about getting started each morning, and he had his animals cared for, fed and bedded down in plenty of time for a cocktail and dinner at each night's stop. Most of all he had the enjoyment of seeing Vermont scenes at a pace unknown by most travelers in the Green Mountain state.

His biggest problem was to find stabling for the animals within reasonable distance of the taverns and inns he had selected. The first night they were put up in a stable run by the inn. The second night he sheltered them in a barn used for horses a mile or so distant from the inn of his choice and which he himself had prepared for them in advance. The third night he put them in an unused barn on the grounds of the inn where he would stay—again fixing up the stalls himself in advance. The fourth night they reached their destination, the Green Mountain Horse Association's headquarters in South Woodstock, where Davisson was to take part in a driving clinic and competition over the weekend.

This was just one drive of many that were held in 1976, ranging from the simple picnic drive of one individual and his passengers to those of driving clubs in Connecticut, Col-

orado, California and many other states. One of the major
beauties of horse and carriage transportation is that you can
get off the beaten path. Using care and common sense a
horse can pull you into invitingly remote areas far from
highways and even byways. After all, horse-drawn vehicles
made the roads for much of this nation's early history—
these same wheel tracks in many cases now paved over for
the benefit of the automobile today.

Two California Drives

California horse and carriage devotees spend much of their
organized time on scenic drives. They haul their horses and
carriages vast miles on the freeways just to get away from it
all on a remote ranch or in a national park. On October 30,
1976 they gathered 18 strong at Yosemite National Park
and here is their own brief description of what must have
been a delightful weekend:

"Some came early and some came late and many travelled
many miles to enjoy one of the best drives of the year on the
Valley Floor of the Park. Stabling was great—upon arrival
everyone found a clean tie stall for his horse with oat hay in
the rack, and the stable manager greeting us with a smile.

32. Littlejohn—a crossbred gelding out of a draft mare—enjoys a picnic
drive put to a wagonette driven by his owner Angela Seabrook. Littlejohn
is a frequent winner in driving competition.

As we collected at the stable or registration desk, we greeted one another, got acquainted and immediately started planning for the coming day's drive. The Park Service was ready for us, providing us with our own, private tour guide from the Park Ranger's office.

"What a lovely drive we had, making the longest possible loop—14 miles in all. The morning was a bit cool and it was cool in the shade, just a bit nippy. Some wore long johns and all had on jackets but the weather was just perfect. The fall colors were beautiful and we had our pictures taken many times as we travelled along to Sentinel Beach for lunch. The trip from the gate through the woods on a road covered with pine needles to picnic tables under the trees was just super! After lunch we journeyed back to the stables, arriving at 3:30, in time to take care of the horses and head for the cabins (which were very nice accommodations) to change clothes in preparation for our dinner at the cafeteria (which served very good food). Some of our group took in the Ranger's evening program at Yosemite Lodge. Sunday some of us went out on another drive, others saddled their horses and rode the Mirror Lake trail.

"For those of you [this account was published in the January, 1977 newsletter of the California Carriage Foundation] who didn't go on this trip you will find 18 persons who can tell you what you missed, so start making plans for next year."

This was just one weekend in the life of the Californians. On November 6, 1976 some of these and others gathered at the happily-named Splinter Bar Farm of John Jenkel in the Sebastopol Hills for an afternoon drive "on local back roads and over hill and dale." A barbecued chicken dinner followed. The next day the group drove from the ranch to the Occidental Union Hotel, a landmark inn amidst the famed Redwoods, where they "feasted" before returning to the starting point.

It is interesting to look at the vehicles used in these two drives. In the two reports the most familiar vehicular term appearing is "buggy." Candidly, many people use the words "buggy" and/or "wagon" to cover all horse-drawn vehicles. Not having been at the California drives this writer can't say whether the "sturdy umbrella buggy" driven by one whip was a true Concord buggy or was a phaeton with a parasol top, but it doesn't matter. The general picture we get from these reports is of a light four-wheeled vehicle—unless more specifically identified—and this seems an indication of geographic preference. In the East the same sort of picnic drive would see many more two-wheeled carts of the Long Island group discussed in the "Two-Wheelers" chapter.

At Yosemite Park three of the vehicles were described as buggies. Another was given as a trap, and a Concord stage coach carried seven members of the party. In the drive through the Redwoods we counted six "buggies," as well as a surrey, a dog cart (four-wheeled), a "pleasure cart," a two-wheeled jogging cart, plus several heavier vehicles pulled by pairs and a four-in-hand.

The point here being that, as we have said before, many vehicles can be used in pleasure driving through the countryside and that one doesn't have to have one particular vehicle for the purpose; in fact, most vehicles were built for just that purpose. Of course one would not take a park-type vehicle such as a Victoria or a Brougham on a picnic drive (nor would one drive a natural wood East Williston cart to a formal wedding involving bridal gowns with trains and grooms with tail coats). Part of the joy of driving with others lies in the variety of vehicles rolling along with yours.

OTHER DRIVING FUN

One cold and windy weekend in 1976 a small group of driving people traveled some 13 miles on horseback to a shelter in a western Connecticut park where they spent the night.

In every case the ridden horses were their favorite driving animals. One wheeled vehicle, a light four-wheeled business, or delivery, wagon pulled by a single Hackney horse, also made the trip—piled high with hay, grain, bedrolls, food for the riders' meals, etc. The next day with hay, grain and food consumed, the wagon was taken to the park's edge and left while the horse between the shafts was unharnessed and saddled for a trail ride to a scenic lookout high in the park. Driving your riding horse and riding your driving horse—this two-way use of your equine friend adds so much to the relationship.

Spectators arriving at such events as polo games, hunt races and horse shows in horse-drawn vehicles generally meet warm welcomes, in fact they add color and excitement to the primary event. While entire parties are sometimes seen at such events atop such vehicles as drags and breaks, the single horse put to a two-wheeled cart is a familiar sight at hunt races in the rolling Pennsylvania countryside—and no doubt at other spots as well. Often special areas at these events are reserved for the carriages which are then used as viewing points by those in them. Picnic hampers are, of course, understood and appreciated.

Sleigh Rides

Long after carriages had been consigned to the dump or left to rot back of the barn, sleighs remained stored or otherwise sheltered. In the beginning it was from a distrust of the motor car's ability to cope with winter. I remember a physician cousin who made winter night house calls in a sleigh pulled by his summertime riding horse rather than risk his fancy open touring car on hilly Berkshire roads. There were many others like him across the country. And there always were those who related winter's fun to jingle bells and sleigh rides.

As the result of this, it is much easier to find sleighs, par-

33. A Canadian-type hunting horse put to an Albany-type cutter.

ticularly of the single-seat or cutter type, at sales, in antique shops and auction halls than to find carriages. Many of them are in surprisingly good shape, needing a bit of paint and some upholstering at the most. A gay blanket or a fur robe can cover a lot of frayed cushions without any further expense or labor. And because use of single-bob and double-bob sleighs is very limited in this era of high-speed winter sanding and plowing, prices are much lower for good antique sleighs than for wheeled vehicles. Prices of from $100 to $250 will buy a sleigh in sound condition.

The two most common types of pleasure sleighs in the United States are the plain-Jane type known as the "Portland" stemming from its Maine origin in the shop of Peter Kimball (1816), and the "Albany." Originally designed and manufactured by James Gould of Albany, N.Y., (1813) this type is marked by graceful and rounded outlines in contrast to the stark, no-nonsense lines of the Portlands. "Swell bodied" is a variation of the Albany cutter or two-seated sleighs, "egg-shell" is another. A third type seen particularly in the Northeast are the several varieties of Canadian sleighs, some of which never have been out of use.

About 20 years ago some fox hunting enthusiasts found their sport cut off abruptly by an early Connecticut winter. Casting about for an outlet for the energies of their hunting horses and bored by the prospect of no more riding until spring, these horsemen proposed to gather on the polo field at Farmington, Connecticut, with their hunters pulling sleighs. The founders of this sport—the late Henry Hoppe of Avon, Connecticut, and Clarence Ambler, then of Woodbury, Connecticut, and more recently of Kennebunk, Maine,—were more than pleased when a dozen or so rigs appeared. Thus the sleigh rally was born.

The sleigh rally provides a blend of nostalgia, pageantry and open air which is exciting to participant and spectator alike. Typical are the rallies held most years by the Wimler family in Durham, Connecticut, where up to 75 rigs circle around a large flat meadow near a state highway. In the center of the circle various classes, similar to those of a driving show or horse show, are called and judged. On the perimeter are a half-dozen or so big flatbed sleighs filled with hay and pulled by heavy draft horse teams of from two to eight horses. The appearance of these in the meadow is a signal for "kids" of all ages—from babes in arms to their grandmothers—to climb aboard for an old-fashioned sleigh ride. Up to 4,000 spectators have been counted at a Durham rally; at historic Johnsonville in East Haddam, Connecticut, in February of 1978, 7,000 were counted and state police estimated they turned away 3,500 more.

In the last few years rallies have been held in Massachusetts, New York State and in Canada. The New England

Region, Carriage Association of America, also stages an annual rally in Jaffrey, New Hampshire. It is difficult to set a formal schedule due to the uncertainties of winter weather, but given the right combination of snow on the meadows, plowed roads and a sunny winter's afternoon these rallies, which are open to all, offer everyone on hand a great deal of pleasure.

In this look at driving for fun we have purposely not discussed the use of your horse in parades or pageants simply because they are no place for beginning drivers. No matter how well-trained your horse, getting involved with crowds, brass bands, floats and the like is difficult enough for the experienced professional, but highly dangerous for the unskilled newcomer. However, as we have seen, there is ample driving for fun all about us—without parades and such. Much of this is available through driving organizations— more on this in the next chapter, but some of the best is that that you and just a few friends can organize yourselves.

7

Organizations

DRIVING PEOPLE, like people of most other inclinations, tend to band together for mutual enjoyment and
support, and sometimes sympathy. One hundred years ago
there were coaching clubs in the major eastern cities; there
were clubs devoted to tandem driving and clubs for
amateur harness racing; there was even a ladies' four-in-
hand club in Manhattan. Long Island was the home of several clubs active in the sport of driving and in many cities
there were driving clubs which became less a matter of driving and more social as the automobile replaced the horse
and carriage. Time and attrition gradually doomed the
others.

A REGIONAL REVIVAL

Today, a new generation of driving organizations born
within the last 15 years holds the loyalties of many driving
people. Most of these are composed of members living
within a regional radius; for example, the Mid-Hudson
Driving Association draws on members from Dutchess and
Ulster counties in New York State, with a few outlying
members from Westchester County and adjoining western
Connecticut locales. Similarly, the Red Rose Horse and

Pony Club finds almost all its members in the area around
Lancaster, Pennsylvania. Perhaps the largest club in numbers is the New England Region Carriage Association of
America, with a membership of approximately 300 in the six
New England states and eastern New York; the largest in
area represented is the California Carriage Foundation,
with its membership of approximately 230 scattered across
the entire Golden Gate state and parts of Nevada.

Other regional clubs are springing up rapidly. Some of
them are in the formative stage, with activities, in the main,
consisting of several picnic drives a year, plus one or more
get-togethers for socializing, showing films of their activities
and exchanges of information. Many more clubs are secure
enough to venture into holding at least one show each year,
and many also schedule clinics for their membership.

Among the groups staging major shows is the Pittsford
Carriage Association located in a suburb of Rochester, New
York. There a dedicated group of sporting drivers annually
stages what is considered a model driving show encompassing three days of competition for both light and draft
horses. Mid-Hudson's 1977 schedule included clinics, a
one-day show for three levels of competitors, an all-day picnic drive on the roads at Lake Mohonk, New York, and a
team competition in combined driving—an event they
pioneered with the Hunterdon Riding and Driving Club of
Flemington, New Jersey. On the West Coast, the California
Foundation specializes in picnic drives in scenic country, but
its members are also found in the driving classes of many
district fairs and shows, including the annual state fair at
Sacramento.

THE NATIONAL SCENE

Two national driving societies invite membership. These are
the Carriage Association of America (CAA), and the Ameri-

can Driving Society (ADS). Beyond that, the American Horse Shows Association has a special committee directed to driving activities.

The CAA

The Carriage Association of America came into being in 1960. The association's quarterly publication, *The Carriage Journal*, gives initial credit to Mrs. C. Grafton Carlisle of the Shelburne Museum in Vermont. As early as 1956 Mrs. Carlisle is reported to have suggested that modern carriage enthusiasts should get together in some kind of organization, pointing out that there was a need for expert advice in the many facets of harness, restoration, and the history of the carriage era. She contacted many people about formation of a horse-drawn vehicle association and received some encouragement. But the idea lay dormant for much of the next four years, until January 28, 1960 when sportsman Ward Melville, trustee of the Suffolk Museum and Carriage House at Stony Brook, Long Island, hosted an organizational luncheon in New York City. Thirteen carriage enthusiasts attended and elected officers. Later that year the group held what was to be its first annual convention at the Suffolk Museum with 29 persons registered in attendance.

Except for an annual meeting devoted to discussion of mutual interest and problems regarding the history and restoration of carriages, the CAA moved slowly until June, 1962 when president Sidney Latham of Texas, announced publication of *The Carriage Journal* to the membership, which by then had grown to a total of 84. In his announcement, he wrote: "We will cater to those who love the memory of that historic age when horse-drawn vehicles fulfilled so many needs of mankind," and then continued, "We have a genuine and sincere affection for the time when new varnish on a rolling carriage wheel seemed to have a brighter sheen than on anything else; the time when the beat of four iron-shod feet on hard clay produced a classic rhythm; the time when the pace of life was fast enough; the time when people depended upon people—and horses—instead of government. We propose that this era not be permitted to die; that its virtues be reaffirmed; that the utilitarian and elegant carriages be preserved as a symbol of its life and living."

Many, if not all, of the original members of the CAA had known the earlier days of coaching and carriage driving. Many of them were collectors of antique carriages, harness and memorabilia of the horse and carriage age, others were students of the history of that period. Still more were artisans devoted to restoration. One of the leading figures was Colonel Paul H. Downing, a life-long resident of Staten Island, New York. Downing, a retired Army officer, had grown up in the carriage age and was considered among the most knowledgeable in the traditions of driving and coaching on the American side of the Atlantic. He was also recognized as the leading authority on vehicle restoration and all the amenities surrounding the elegant carriage, its occupants and its horses—and was an obvious choice for editor of *The Carriage Journal.*

For the next decade Downing reigned as a virtual czar over the affairs of the CAA through his post as editor. His contributions and dedication to driving and the association were unquestioned, but his scorn for any deviation from the high degree of elegance he demanded irritated many, frightened others and may, through this attitude, have stifled some of the budding interest in driving. Downing was not interested in competition driving nor did he look upon *The Carriage Journal* as a news publication. Aside from notices of events directly concerning the CAA, he gave drives and shows short shrift. Nevertheless, he survived several internal rifts in the early days of the organization, and in spite of any reservations was ultimately a definite factor in the steady growth of the membership lists. Toward the end of his editorship ill health took him out of the active scene; and for the last several years of his life, he conducted the affairs of *The Carriage Journal* from his bed overlooking the carriage house where he had, years earlier, learned about driving at his father's knee. Living in the past, Downing failed to understand, or compromise with, the groundswell toward relaxation of the established driving code, and the magazine, of course, reflected that attitude.

Nevertheless the Carriage Association continued to grow and prosper under the careful guidance of a succession of presidents and the dedicated direction of a noted collector, Horace K. Sowles, Jr. of Portland, Maine, who became secretary-treasurer. By the mid-1970's membership had grown to nearly 3,500 in the United States and abroad. Upon Downing's death in 1975, Sowles convinced Tom Ryder, noted driving professional from Yorkshire, England and author of a number of books and articles on the sport (see bibliography)—and by then manager of the coaching activities of Mr. and Mrs. John Seabrook of Salem, New Jersey—to become the new editor of *The Carriage Journal*.

The annual convention and the quarterly magazine are the two major functions of the CAA. Another plus for the membership is the large listing of books on driving available through the secretary's office (P.O. Box 3788, Portland, Maine 04101).

The ADS

During the 1974 driving competition season a small group of regular competitors disturbed by a lack of uniformity in the rules governing the various driving competitions, and by the lack of attention being paid by the CAA, began talk-

34. Philip Hofmann, founder
and president of the American
Driving Society.

ing about the possibility of forming a new national body to
provide unity and direction to the sport of driving for
pleasure. Late in that season letters were sent to 50 of the
most dedicated competitors in the country calling for a
meeting to be held at Stony Brook—interestingly enough,
the site of the first CAA convention as well—during the
weekend of the annual Suffolk Museum and Carriage
House competition. A total of 40 positive responses, with a
commitment of $100 each, were counted and an election of
officers was held, with Philip Hofmann, an international
competitor and judge from New Brunswick, New Jersey,
being chosen as the first president of the newly-named
American Driving Society.

Whereas the CAA had a specific interest in carriages—
with the driving of them only one aspect—the ADS im-

mediately concentrated its attention on the driving sport itself. Instituting a single set of rules for competitions in this country was one immediate goal; the education of drivers in the sport was another. The first issue of *The Whip*, the official newsletter of the new society, was dated January, 1975, with this writer as editor. Unlike *The Carriage Journal*, the new ADS publication concentrated on news of events, results of shows, a calendar of scheduled events and other items of both general and individual interest. In 1976, *The Whip* was published nine times. Also in that year, a handbook containing the Society's bylaws and standards for competitions was published for the first time. A second and revised edition—containing a list of judges approved by the ADS and the American Horse Shows Association, as well as a section devoted to the organization and operation of competitions—was issued early in 1977. This handbook is still available at the society's central office in care of Robert Heath, 339 Warburton Avenue, Hastings-on-Hudson, New York 10706.

The ADS meets annually for an autumn weekend of driving, picnics and other allied activities on the reservation of the Mohonk Mountain House at Lake Mohonk in New Paltz, New York where there are 45 miles of dirt roads exclusively for horses and carriages. In addition, each year the society conducts at least one clinic for judges and student judges, while officers of the society assist smaller clubs and informal groups with the operation of shows and clinics. By early 1977, membership in the American Driving Society had passed the 800 mark, and the announced goal of 1,000 members was reached in September of 1977.

The AHSA

The American Horse Shows Association, by far the largest equine-based organization in the world, has a driving committee. In 1977, it endorsed the rules of the ADS, thus insuring a single set of regulations for pleasure competitions in this country. This, however, is not to be confused with the "pleasure" divisions in the various breed driving classes such as those run by the Morgan, Arabian and Quarter Horse breed associations. The ADS does not attempt to regulate inring breed driving competitions.

INTERNATIONALLY SPEAKING

The British Driving Society

The British Driving Society, which numbers members in this country and others, as well as in its home islands, has district commissioners in every county of England, Wales, Scotland and northern Ireland and each sponsors picnic drives, competitions and clinics. In addition, a combined driving organization has been set up within the B.D.S.

Americans may join the British Driving Society for an annual membership of five pounds. They may be reached c/o Mrs. P. Chandler, secretary, 10 Marley Ave., New Milton, Hampshire, England.

The FEI

The Fédération Équestre Internationale, or FEI, is the governing body of international horse sports, excluding racing and polo. It came into being in the 1950's, with its headquarters established in Switzerland, and its goal the encouragement and control of top flight competition among the riders of the world. At the very top of the competition ladder are the international events held under its rules. The FEI established driving rules after its president, Prince Philip of England, was made aware of the intense interest in driving events existing in several of the European countries. Early in the 1970's the establishment of a world championship every other year was authorized by the FEI which found, to its delight, that its own president was to be an enthusiastic competitor.

As we shall see in the "Combined Driving" chapter, FEI driving competitions were at first confined to four-in-hands. In fact, although there has been some opening up of FEI events to single and pairs at the national and local level, the international emphasis is still with the four-in-hands.

Combined driving competition is the focus of FEI driving activity. These competitions consist of a program of three distinct phases: Dressage and Presentation constituting Competition A; Cross-country, Competition B; and Obstacle Driving, Competition C. Although a very challenging and exciting event for advanced horsemen—and spectators—FEI combined driving events are very difficult to stage, chiefly due to the intricacies of scoring which necessitate even more people "on the ground" than are competing, plus the large amount of real estate required on which to conduct the cross-country phase.

In the United States, this kind of combined-driving event was introduced in 1970 by Philip Hofmann, then chairman of the board of the Johnson & Johnson Company. Hofmann, the same Hofmann who later would become the first president of the American Driving Society, was one of a handful of Americans who had competed abroad. Although he had more than one team of four in his own barns, he opened the competition up to singles and pairs, recognizing that there were not enough fours in this country to make a show possible. However, after a second year, the FEI competition at Johnson Park in New Brunswick was, sadly, dropped.

It's clear from even this brief chapter on driving organizations that, despite some problems, the driving-for-sport scene is becoming more and more active each year both in North America and abroad.

8

Leading Events

THE INCREASING interest in pleasure driving which manifested itself in the middle-1970's was reflected by a similar increase in the number of competitions appearing on the calendar of equine sporting events.

In 1970 there were only a handful of all-driving events held, and these were not annual fixtures. Among the pioneer events were the two FEI programs staged at Johnson Park at New Brunswick, New Jersey, under the direction of Philip Hofmann, several one-day competitive drives at the St. Peter's Village restoration near Pottstown, Pennsylvania, and scattered shows in New England. These were open to the public. A handful of invitational drives were held at sporadic intervals in the New Jersey–Philadelphia area and in that same general geographical region there was the annual "marathon" staged in conjunction with the Devon Horse Show, plus a gathering of coaching-carriage devotees at many of the hunt races there.

But the interest in driving competitions grew steadily as more and more horsemen rediscovered the pluses in the combination of horse and carriage, and gradually new competitive events emerged.

ANNUAL SHOWS

The Fairfield Show

Among the early shows which did become "annual" and survived for a lengthy period was that held each summer at the Fairfield County Hunt Club in the Connecticut town of Westport. It was conceived and motivated by Mrs. Barbara Brewster Taylor, daughter and granddaughter of presidents of Brewster & Company, the outstanding carriage makers. A lifelong sportswoman and horsewoman, the indomitable Mrs. Taylor was in her late seventies when she staged the first show in 1972 with the assistance of this writer, and even later when she turned over much of the work to her daughter, Marie Frost, Mrs. Taylor remained the spark plug for the event into her eighties.

There were a number of factors which made the Fairfield competition a continuing success. The Hunt Club facilities are designed to entertain and enhance equine sports. Many of its members are active as fox hunters, polo players and horse show exhibitors. The spacious clubhouse, porch and lawn make an ideal location from which to view action on the big polo field—a field highly suitable for carriage competitions. There is an experienced staff in both stables and clubhouse. Covered riding arenas protect the competition vehicles at night. More than that, the community understands and appreciates what goes on in a driving show since gracious living is a part of the suburban Fairfield County life and the elegance of the horses and carriages seen at Fairfield each year reflects that way of life. The sporting bent of the community brings forth willing helpers to assist the committee as we saw at the 1977 show headed by Miss

Frost and poloist Thomas Glynn. In addition, the geographical location some 50 miles more or less from mid-
Manhattan puts this show near the center of eastern carriage activity.

The Stony Brook Show

Another annual carriage event of similar background and
format was that at the North Shore Horse Show grounds at
Stony Brook, Long Island, for the benefit of the Suffolk
Museum and Carriage House. The area is similar to
Fairfield's; indeed, as the crow flies, Stony Brook is directly
opposite Westport across Long Island Sound. The show
grounds, with ring, spacious outside course used for hunter
classes at under-saddle horse shows, and permanent stabling lie less than 100 yards from the shore. A covered grand-
stand overlooks the ring and a nearby clubhouse is available
for social affairs connected with the driving activities.

Stony Brook's place in the carriage picture was solidified
by its connections with the museums in the village where the
Carriage House holds what is regarded as one of the
superior collections of horse-drawn vehicles in the United
States. The show's honorary chairman was the late Ward
Melville, first president of the Carriage Association of
America, who founded the museums, though direction of
the two-day competition from the beginning was handled by
Mr. Melville's daughter and son-in-law, Mr. and Mrs. James
Blackwell, even as Miss Frost functions for her mother at
Fairfield.

The Pittsford Show

A third "venerable" annual competition is that started in
1972 in the western New York State town of Pittsford, a
suburb of Rochester. Here school teacher William Remley,

who serves as president of the Pittsford Carriage Club and is active in the American Driving Society, holds an ambitious program of some 40-plus classes over three days at his Walnut Hill Farm. Remley has instituted a number of innovative classes at Walnut Hill including classes for draft animals and vehicles which get the neighboring farmers in that highly agricultural region involved. The Walnut Hill driving competitions have attracted entries from as far away as Ohio and eastern Massachusetts, drawn by Remley's growing fame as a host and show organizer. (Examples of Remley's ingenuity will be found in the chapter on rules.)

Other Annual Events

Several other local driving clubs hold ambitious annual competitions. The New England chapter of the Carriage Association of America held one-day shows at North Andover, Massachusetts for three years, and in 1977 increased its schedule, with action starting at noon on Saturday and continuing throughout Sunday. The Lincoln and Carriage Club in Arcola, Illinois combines three days of driving competition with visits to Amish harness and carriage shops and farms. The Mid-Hudson Driving Club staged a one-day driving competition for all levels at the Dutchess County fairgrounds in Rhinebeck, New York, in 1978 after inaugurating team competition in 1976 with the Hunterdon Horse and Pony Club in New Jersey, which also annually holds a full day's schedule of competitive classes.

In Maryland the Harford County Equestrian Center scheduled its fourth annual driving competition in June of 1978. An expanded promotion in Connecticut was that at the equestrian center of The Kent School with more than 40 classes at all levels scheduled for the Labor Day weekend in 1977. Ohioans listed action at the Mid-American Coaching and Driving competition at Mentor later in September, while devotees in the Delmarva region were summoned to meets at Morven Park in Leesburg, Virginia and at Oakdale Farm in Rockville, Maryland in October.

"MARATHONS"

For the first few years the formats at the pioneering Fairfield and Stony Brook meets included a "marathon" on the third day. In the true sense of the word these were not marathons at all, but road drives during which entries were judged in much the same manner as were pleasure classes in the ring, some attention being paid to manners of the horses on the road and a veterinary inspection of the animals at the finish. The distances were moderate, generally not more than 10 miles, and with a liberal maximum time to complete the drive allowed.

The Devon Drive

These were modeled after the historic Devon coaching marathon in Pennsylvania held each Memorial Day weekend as part of the famed Devon Horse Show. As a "happening" the Devon marathon is without peer. It began in the horse and buggy era as a strictly four-in-hand event, open only to park drags and road coaches. Shortly after World War II it lapsed into limbo as those big rigs remained unhorsed in the carriage barns of the Philadelphia area Main Liners and the few other coaching buffs in the country. It was revived in 1966 when Henry Collins III and several other Devon enthusiasts opened the marathon to all comers; a decade later entries had swelled to more than 80 individual coaches, carriages and carts of all descriptions.

But the Devon drive, with all its wonderful blend of color, high society, nostalgia and excitement, is not a true

35. Mr. and Mrs. Nathaniel Pulsifer of Ipswich, Massachusetts, preparing for a cross-country marathon competition in Vermont. He greases one of the wheels while she figures the speed they should make over the course.

marathon or is it even a fair test of road driving. Entries are prejudged at the assembly point with emphasis on suitability, appointments and elegance. They then are driven four and one-half miles in a procession on hard roads to the Devon show grounds and come into the famed Wanamaker Oval where they are pinned before the crowds in the covered stands. First and second place winners in each division then return to the ring for the championship, after which the entries go back individually to the starting point and disperse. Nowhere else in the western hemisphere is there such an annual spectacle of horses, vehicles and whips.

Starting in 1975, suggestions for the "improvement" of the Devon marathon have been heard with increasing frequency. The consensus among the "hard driving" crowd is that a driving competition at various levels should precede the "marathon," thus giving competitors from lengthy distances a worthwhile program. Supporters of this idea point out that whereas the original coaching marathon drew most of its entries from the New York–Philadelphia corridor, present-day entries come from as far away as Ohio and Missouri and the North Shore of Massachusetts, and that a single 40-minute, four-mile drive isn't enough to justify the expenditure of time and money. On the side of the traditionalists, and the dedicated people who run the Devon show, there just isn't room or time for a big carriage competition in the present format of the biggest and best outdoor horse show in the country. This writer believes that the answer lies in a separately-operated carriage meet held close by a day or two before the present marathon. This should satisfy all involved, and would preserve, if not actually enhance, the frame and artistry of the Devon Marathon..

Be that as it may, in 1977 both Fairfield and Stony Brook dropped their climaxing road "marathons" in favor of more tests of driving skills on their grounds. This put an end to the annual cocktail parties and luncheons held along the routes by adjacent homeowners who invited friends to "watch the carriages go by," but it kept the spectators on the grounds and it saved the animals miles of trotting travel on hard and slippery macadam.

COMBINED DRIVING EVENTS

But the enthusiastic long-distance driver was finding a new outlet for the energies of his horses under the rules of the

Federation Equestre Internationale. Even as the combined form of three-day *riding* events were becoming more and more popular in the second half of the 1970's so were combined driving events.

The cross-country (Competition B) section of the combined driving event has become known as the "marathon." In the World or European championships for four-in-hands the distances are as much as 26 miles. In this country, where competitions are open to all sorts of entries, from wee single Shetlands to massive four-in-hands, distances have been kept to less than 20 miles, and some cross-country courses have been a lot shorter. But cross-country is all the name implies—rigorous.

As we saw earlier, the pioneer FEI event in this country was that staged by Philip Hofmann in 1970. In 1974, Victor and Evelyn Shone, operators of Shone's Driving Establishment in Millbrook, New York staged a full-fledged combined driving competition under FEI rules. The event was well-received and they were encouraged to repeat in 1975. They held their fourth annual FEI meet in 1977. However, at this writing the future does not look bright for this fine event. The time, energy and money required to put on an event of this caliber are taking their toll.

As of mid-1978 the leading FEI driving promotion in the United States is that held for five times at Hamilton, Massachusetts, under the spirited and knowledgeable direction of Mrs. Robert Pirie of Hamilton, and Mrs. Nathanial Pulsifer of Ipswich. Their first Myopia Three-Day Driving Event was held in 1976 at the Myopia Hunt and Polo Club, the enclave made nationally famous by Boston-based socialites and sportsmen. They have been offering FEI "by the book" ever since. They pioneered the first (and only) FEI competition for four-in-hand entries in October of 1977, attracting 14 original teams of which only five managed to finish. In June of 1978 they attracted 51 entries to their competition with a distinguished panel of U.S.-based experts accredited to the FEI and international judges from Britain and Canada.

Mrs. Pirie and Mrs. Pulsifer and a number of their leading assistants have spent much time in England and Europe at driving events. There is little doubt that the British and European drivers are far ahead of the Americans. For one thing, from the Irish Sea to the Crimea and the Black Sea horse sports remain second only to soccer in spectator interest and understanding. Twenty-one teams of four-in-hands entered the 1978 British championships held at Windsor Castle. There were better than 40 four-in-hands at the sparkling international horse extravaganza at Aachen in West Germany.

Even as they fail to appreciate polo, steeplechasing and combined riding events, American spectators fall far behind their European counterparts in appreciation of driving. The largest crowd ever to see any part of driving was that at Ledyard in the Myopia country in 1976: 30,000 attended, but—rather than to watch the carriages—to see Princess Anne of Great Britain and her husband competing in the stadium jumping section of the Horse Trials just prior to the Olympics.

The "ladies of Myopia" are determined to bring combined driving front and center among American horse sports. They have competed abroad, have officiated at international competitions in England and Europe, have studied at first hand the rules-making procedures of the FEI. More, they have an experienced and dedicated corps of timers, referees and other officials fast learning to handle the intricacies of scoring and placing entries. Their enthusiasms easily intrigue leading Europeans into coming to America as judges, officials and teachers.

Even as one or two combined driving competitions falter, new ones appear. At Gladstone, New Jersey, home of the

United State Equestrian Team's dressage and jumping teams, a full-fledged competition for drivers was conducted most successfully in 1977. The 1978 date was by-passed, but plans already are well underway for the 1979 competition. New in 1978 was a combined driving event at the Chester-land Horse Trials in Unionville, Pennsylvania.

OTHER EVENTS—MOSTLY FUN

Among the most enthusiastic whips in the country is George Weymouth of Chadds Ford, Pennsylvania. A one-time captain of polo at Yale and for many years president and director of the Brandywine Polo Club, this dedicated sportsman enjoys nothing more than to load his coach with friends and go for long picnic drives through his fields and those of his neighbors along the Pennsylvania–Delaware border. For several years he has held an invitational meet of four-in-hand whips at his estate, The Big Bend, so named for its location on the banks of the Brandywine River, through which the teams are required to ford at least three times. Weymouth's credo is "fun first and last" and he encourages numerous breaches of FEI rules whenever he feels they restrict pure fun. The three days of driving and the nights of cocktails and dinner at Chadds Ford supply a lifetime of cherished memories to those lucky enough to be invited. The enthusiasm of Weymouth, who is not nicknamed "Frolic" for nothing, sets the pace.

Late in October of 1976 William Davisson—the same Davisson we followed from Marlboro to Woodstock two chapters back and a Vermont college faculty member—ran a cross-country competition under FEI rules, with the help of a handful of young people employed on his Robinson–Winchester Farm in Marlboro, Vermont. Despite problems of weather and terrain, his event was considered a rousing success by competitors and onlookers alike, thus encouraged, he scheduled a second event for 1977—a second in what is hoped will become an annual event.

In addition to the all-driving competitions and the FEI events, numerous established horse shows have recognized the increasing interest in driving by adding some driving classes to their ridden fixtures. For several years the annual Children's Services Horse Show in the Hartford, Connecticut, suburb of Farmington has featured a road drive where entries are prejudged, to be looked at again during a drive of six miles or so enroute to the show grounds at the Farmington Valley Polo Club. There they have their moment in the spotlight as they enter the main ring class by class, are identified to the people in the stands, and then pinned. Many other shows have pleasure classes in the ring. In the 1977 Devon show a new class for pairs to be driven through a serpentine course in the Wanamaker Oval was sponsored by Mr. and Mrs. Philip Hofmann.

The California Carriage Foundation does not run competitions of its own, leaning as it does more to day outings through the scenic countryside, but it has taken a leading role in urging the management of the many county and district fairs, as well as CalExpo, the annual state fair at Sacramento, to offer pleasure driving competitions.

A Great Finale

Annually, the pleasure driving and coaching season in this hemisphere comes to a glittering end under the acres of roof which house the Royal Horse Show, a part of the Royal Winter Agricultural Fair at Toronto. Pleasure driving and obstacle classes for four-in-hands are held before thousands in the main Coliseum there each November, and as a barometer of the mounting interest in both Canada and the U.S.A., pleasure classes for junior drivers and single ponies have now been added to the prize list. In 1978 Mr. J. D. Pemberton, a noted whip, was elected president of this fair.

9

Novice Competitions

U P T O this point we have directed most of our attention to the beginner. In this chapter we will refer to the beginner as the "novice," simply because under the rules which govern driving competition the "novice" category is that for drivers and horses in their first competitive experiences in the ring or going cross-country.

But, before the "beginner" becomes a "novice," we would suggest that he drive his horse in the home atmosphere—meadow and road—until he has acquired some much-needed confidence in himself and his horse, and until the basics of harnessing and driving become second nature. Meanwhile the beginner turning novice would do well to attend as many driving competitions as he can. And having riding-show experience helps too. Try to assimilate the show ring routine by observation before you come face to face with it in your first competition. And if you are interested enough and lucky enough, there is a chance that some whip will offer you a ride during a pleasure class so you may see what the inside of a driving arena looks like from the seat of a carriage.

THE "RING"/ARENA

For driving competition in general the word "ring" is somewhat misleading. While most breed classes are held in the show ring, the pleasure driving competitions more often take place in more open spaces. In fact, there are some very precise dimensions suggested under certain rules for certain types of competition. Driven dressage, for instance, is to be conducted in an area 330 feet by 132 feet, if that much space is available. This is twice as large as most show rings and rectangular in shape instead of oval. A somewhat smaller dressage arena the same width but 264-feet long is allowed when judging singles and pairs in their dressage tests.

Many shows use the dressage arena for all pleasure classes as well. While there is a suggestion in the rules of both the American Driving Society and the American Horse Shows Association—these, as of January 1, 1977, are identical for pleasure driving competitions (not to be confused with the "pleasure" divisions of the breed shows)—that a continuous fence should be provided for the dressage arena, in reality many are outlined simply with traffic cones, ridden dressage corners connected by lines of lime or sawdust, or by very low boards similar to those used in outdoor polo. If used at all, the familiar show ring of the ridden horse is used for pleasure classes and driving tests, but these generally are felt to be too small, thus inhibiting the free movement considered so ideal for the carriage horse.

Novices wishing to practice the driving tests outlined in this chapter can easily set up an area in any available meadow by pacing off four sides and putting a simple flag

36. New Yorker (state, that is) Diane Huber behind her crossbred pony put to a pony village cart at a Milbrook, New York, competition.

or marker of any kind at each corner and then driving within the imaginary bounds delineated by those markers.

TODAY'S CLASSES

Competition driving moved rapidly in the first half of the 1970's. From a simple driving class at a local horse show judged, in the main, by "old timers" who professed knowledge of "how it used to be when I was a boy," the sport now numbers more than 50 all-driving competitions in the United States and many uncounted more in Canada. Rules for such competitions were written and adopted by the ADS and the AHSA in 1976 and revised in 1977. Judges were trained at clinics and recognized on official lists. In 1977 the ADS began to "recognize" competitions, and the standardization of prize lists and specifications for classes became widespread.

Pleasure Driving for Single Horses

The first class likely to attract the novice is the simple pleasure driving class for single horses. But, before he drives his horse through the in-gate for the first time, the novice must understand a number of basic requirements. His horse must be clean and so must his harness. The driver should wear a hat, gloves and a driving apron or robe. Unless the prize list specifically permits the use of a "bicycle-wheeled" vehicle, such as the modern jogger, the vehicle must be traditional in design with wooden wheels.

The horse may be of any breed or a crossbred. There is no limitation as to color, and size is only defined by the rule which states that a horse must be over 14.2 unless he is of the exempt breeds such as the Morgan, Arab and Standardbred where a purebred animal 14.2 or under may compete in the horse classes; otherwise the animal must compete in the pony division. Good conformation and way of going as well as the other attributes listed below will be considered by the judges. Manes may be braided or not.

In this class all entries enter the ring or arena and are judged one against the other on the basis of performance, suitability and quality of the complete turnout. At command, the entries will move at the walk, collected trot, working trot, trot-on, and will be asked to halt, back up and stand quietly.

The Standards For Competitions of the ADS (and the ASHA) describe the *walk* as being free-moving, flat-footed and brisk. The driver should maintain light contact on the horse's mouth. The book suggests that judges study the walk while the turnout is reversing diagonally across the ring.

The *collected trot* is slow and "the animal is to be kept together, cadence to be sharp and balanced with the hindquarters well engaged, head nicely flexed, a little in front of vertical. The horse should be happy in the mouth and contact should be light."

The *working trot* sees the horse showing a freer movement with a smooth transition from the collected trot and a slight lengthening of the stride while still under light contact.

The *trot-on* gait should be faster, well-balanced with a longer stride. The horse's head should be flexed around the turns, and should not point to the outside in the turns; nor should he be leading with his inside shoulder. Light contact is required and breaking stride or excessive speed are penalized in the scoring.

In some classes an *extended trot* may be asked. This involves lengthening of the stride without increasing the pace, the hindquarters to be engaged as in the collected trot and with the cadence of the collected trot maintained without lengthening of head and neck, or loss of contact.

With all the horses and vehicles lined up in the center, each entry is asked to *back up* at least four steps unhurried, with head and neck straight, pushing back with the hindquarters. Contact should be light and the voice low, if used at all. Then, the horse should step quietly forward into his original position and halt. A groom is permitted at the horse's head, but should not hold the horse except in the case of unruliness which might lead to an accident or runaway.

This class is judged as follows: the horse counts 50 per cent on the basis of manners, way of going, condition, suitability or appropriateness and backing. The driver counts for

20 per cent, use of aids and posture being noted particularly. The fit, condition and appropriateness of the harness counts for 15 per cent and the fit, condition and appropriateness of the vehicle for another 15.

The word "appropriate" as applied to the harness and the vehicle means that the size and type of vehicle and harness must go together with the horse. The harness should be in good repair, clean and fit properly; all metal hardware should match, be secure and polished. The vehicle should be sound, balanced and appear pleasant. Brown or russet harness is appropriate with vehicles of natural wood finish, black harness with painted vehicles. For most of the light American sporting vehicles breast collars are acceptable; round or full collars are appropriate to heavier carriages.

The Whip

The book maintains that "whips (drivers) must be dressed conservatively in the style of the day." What was great in Grandma's day is considered a costume now and is not permitted. Judges would frown at feathered plumes on Milady's hat. Or hoop skirts. In the other extreme, short skirts for ladies on high vehicles aren't appropriate either, though the driving apron helps in that area. But pantsuits are o.k.

Hats are essential for both men and women. A hat with a large, floppy brim is a hindrance to a lady whip since it obstructs the vision. The novice male may wear a soft felt or straw hat or a gray or black derby (bowler).

A whip must be carried in the right hand at all times. Putting down the whip while driving in competition would be considered a serious flaw in the driver's skill since the whip is an aid, and certainly would result in a loss of much of the 20 per cent given to the driver in pleasure driving classes.

Under ADS rules youngsters who have not reached their 18th birthday at the time of the show can enter junior classes. Some competitions, particularly those with cross-country events, require children under 14 to be accompanied by an adult but this is not mandatory under the existing ADS rules.

Driving Test #1

Until 1976 classes for juniors to drive and ladies to drive, etc., were judged almost identically with the pleasure class just outlined. However, experts in the sport felt that this did not provide enough emphasis on the skill of the driver. So a simple test was devised, varying in demand only with the expertise of the contestant.

Driving test #1 is for the novice, who is defined in the rules as a horse and/or whip who have not won a blue ribbon at any driving event. This is the test for the beginner.

Three markers are placed on the same side of the ring or arena, one at each end and one in the middle. The driver enters the area on the center line and walks his horse to the point opposite the middle marker where he halts his horse and salutes the judge with his whip. (The *whip salute* is given by holding the whip in an upright position and raising the butt end even with the face; or by placing the whip in the left hand and removing the hat. The latter is for men only obviously.)

Once the judge returns the salute the test continues at a working trot, turning right to make a large circle at the end of the arena. At the end of the circle the contestants slow to a walk and pass across to the other end on the diagonal. At the marker a working trot on the left rein starts, making a large circle before going to the side opposite the end marker and crossing the arena once more on the diagonal still at the working trot. The test then turns right at the far marker, thence to the center line and down the center to the middle. There, there's a halt for five seconds and a back-up for four strides; then a return to the middle point, halt, salute and then an exit from the arena down the center line at a walk.

This is a very simple test to practice at home. A word of caution here: don't practice too much because your horse will start doing it on his own, anticipating the turns and changes of gait. "Great!" you say, "if I forget, the horse will know and do it anyway." But invariably the horse makes his moves too soon, cuts his corners, halts before he gets to the middle, etc.

The nine various moves are numbered and each is assigned a points value of 0–10. The winner is the driver with the highest total. The major difference between this driving test and the pleasure driving class is that the judging here is based solely on performance of the nine moves while the pleasure driving class takes into consideration the whole turnout—horse, driver, harness and vehicle, with performance only one of many factors determining the winner. The novice moves along to elementary status in time, and then higher up on the scale to the intermediate category.

Time Classes

Beyond the pleasure driving classes and the driving tests are an entirely different kind of competition in which the novice may take part for they are open to all. These are lumped under the heading of "time classes." In effect they are games played one at a time over the same course for everyone, with the winner to be determined in several different ways according to the game played. In each case a recorder replaces the judge who is not necessary in these events.

OBSTACLE CLASS

The *obstacle* class—many of these games are known by this name though they are not truly obstacle classes—calls for each competitor to drive over a course consisting of 20

37. Scott Hill, Jr. puts a Castle Farm Hackney pony through its paces in the obstacle section of the 1977 Broadmere, New Jersey, Combined Driving event. The vehicle is a cut-under pony cart.

"gates," or "obstacles," formed by placing two traffic cones, or similar markers, in the manner of poles in a skiing slalom race. Each set of gates is adjusted to a predetermined width based on the measurement of the widest point of the carriage to the highest point of the marker. Rules call for clearances of from 6 to 16 inches, the general clearance used is 12 inches. Time is taken from the moment the front axle of the carriage passes the starting line until the axle passes over the finish line. For each marker hit 10 seconds in penalty time is added to the elapsed time. The fastest time wins.

Rule 2.10B governs an obstacle class in which the least number of markers hit determines the winner; if two or more contestants are tied, a drive-off over a shortened course takes place with elapsed time to count as well.

Some general rules for obstacle driving: no one is allowed to drive on the course or lead their horses through the course prior to the competition, but drivers may walk the course themselves. Circling in front of an obstacle and crossing one's own wheel tracks carries a 10-second penalty for each of the first two instances and a third infraction brings elimination. Going off course eliminates the entry, unless the mistake is rectified before going through the next gate. A breakdown of harness or vehicle eliminates the entry. Some competitions prohibit cantering and these require an official to rule on the break in gait. The first two breaks carry penalties of 10 seconds each and the ruling official must be convinced that the driver stopped his horse immediately. The third break from a trot eliminates the entry.

GAMBLERS CHOICE

Gamblers Choice classes are modeled after those popular in the horse show jumping divisions. Whereas the obstacle courses as described in the previous paragraphs are laid out so that the driver must proceed through the gates in order, the Gamblers Choice gates or obstacles are assigned points in the order of their difficulty for the driver, the most difficult being given the highest number of points. The driver has a time limit during which he tries to pile up as many points as possible by going through the most difficult obstacles. He is allowed only two times through each obstacle and he must not go through any one obstacle consecutively, but must attempt a different one before repeating that obstacle again.

Gamblers Choice courses generally are set up in less space than are the obstacle or other time classes. And some of the most difficult obstacles to conquer seem deceptively easy. At the 1976 driving competition of the New England Region Carriage Association of America, the most difficult gate— which even the designers didn't realize would cause much. trouble—turned out to be two fur robes draped over barrels through which the vehicle was to be driven. Many of the horses would have nothing to do with that! Bridges, areas into which the vehicle must be backed, "clotheslines" flying laundry or flags, imitation "water" crossings over newspaper, crates containing live fowl—these are just a few of the many possibilities found in Gamblers Choice competitions. Parallel bars laid on the ground through which the driver must pass without touching, U-turns and twists are other familiar tests in Gamblers Choice.

In the *Progressive* class which is short and quick, the vehicle must pass through six numbered gates composed of markers topped by tennis balls. The first gate gives a clearance of 20 inches with each getting progressively tighter until the last allows a clearance of only two inches. Two points are awarded for each gate cleared. In the event of a tie time taken decides the winner.

The *Fault and Out* class is again modeled after a class by the same name in open jumping. The vehicle proceeds through a numbered series of gates until the time limit is passed or a gate is dislodged. Total points determine the winner and time counts in the event of a tie.

Cross-Country Classes

Some of the bigger competitions are now instituting the *cross-country* class. These are more familiarly known as the mini-marathon, mainly because they resemble the cross-country or marathon phase of the combined driving competitions. Whereas the latter extend as far as 16 miles or more, these mini-marathons often are less than a quarter-mile long, resembling the true cross-country tests only in the types of hazards to be met and passed through. Natural and artificial obstacles are used, such as banks, bridges, water, farm equipment and animals, pens and so forth. A first refusal at a hazard earns three penalty points, the second six penalty points and the third elimination. Knocking down or disturbing an obstacle earns four penalty points and each second taken over the time allowed earns an additional one penalty point. Obviously, lowest score wins.

Marathons under ADS rules, as distinguished from those combined driving competitions governed by the international FEI book, are a drive on the road over a given distance, usually six miles or more, to be completed within a given time. It is not a race, its purpose is to test the training, manners and fitness of the horse and the ability of the driver under conditions normally encountered on the road. Judges observe each entry prior to the drive and see each entry at least once while on the road. Assistant judges are stationed at key locations to assist in evaluating the performances, and most shows have a veterinarian at the finish to report on the fitness of the horse there.

Elegance Classes

The *"Concours d'Elegance"* competitions should be considered generally beyond the reach of the beginner, although conceivably not entirely. These competitions are, as the name in French implies, designed to establish the most elegant turnout on the premises of any driving competition, and the first-year driver who seeks victory in such company is guilty of either wishful thinking or foolhardiness—or perhaps both. Elegant (and expensive) harness and vehicles, plus personal clothing which indicates skill and experience the driver does not have, are not in good taste for the novice. One acquires skills in any sport by much practice with the basic tools; once the skills are mastered then is the time to start climbing the ladder.

The "Concours d'Elegance" competitions are not to be confused with the "Cavalcade Americana" classes of the Morgan breed shows or the "Currier & Ives" classes of the Yankee Rallies and sleighing competitions. The last two are

38. (*Above*). The hunt saddle and lack of regular harness on the lead horse reveal this as a sporting tandem, which evolved as one way to get the hunting horse to the hunt. The driver is owner Mrs. Barbara Weir of Califon, New Jersey, with her son, John, as groom. The vehicle is a tub cart.

39. (*Below*). This snappy pony tandem put to a pony rally cart is driven by Mrs. Basil Steton of Princeton, New Jersey.

Today's class for sporting tandems derives from that scheme. The leader (hunter) is driven in front of a horse and cart, attached to the turnout by reins and traces. He wears hunting tack; i.e., saddle, hunting bridle, sandwich case. Unlike the more formal park tandems which attain much elegance through matched horses, there need be little resemblance between hunter and shaft horse in the sporting variety since appearance was not the original intent. But the hunter in the lead is required to be ridden and may be asked to jump. The groom riding in the vehicle with the hunting man must be able to drive the shaft horse and cart away once the hunter has been detached and mounted.

It is a very colorful class with its own special demands on the training of the horse and the skill of the driver. It involves four reins rather than two, a combination of horse and vehicle length double the normal which poses problems when turning corners, as well as the other problems posed by a leader working out in front virtually "free" except for remote control. Tandem driving is an art best performed by artists. It scares many drivers, which may be just as well. Certainly it is a form of driving for the beginner to watch and appreciate, but not attempt.

Even so, surely the beginning driver will find ample enough challenges in this chapter to keep him well occupied for a goodly time to come.

10

Combined Driving

" E V E N T I N G " is a relatively new word in horse sports. It is short for "combined riding event," an arduous form of equestrian competition built on a format of rigorous exercises—exercises calling for a combination of skill, stamina and courage from both horse and rider and conducted over three days of performance.

THE FEI FORMAT

Eventing, as we know it today at least, is the godchild of the Fédération Équestre Internationale, and its rules, as we shall see, determine much of what happens on the current eventing scene—both ridden and driven.

The eventing format devised in FEI's early years remains unchanged today except in degree. It brings together the combination of dressage—with its precisions of changes in gait and direction—and the strength-draining cross-gallops and jumps of the roads and tracks and steeplechase sections, and culminates in a demanding stadium jumping finale. Conducted over three days in the pure form, this format soon found its nicknames, such as "eventing," "horse trials," and "CTA" (letters standing for the Combined Training Association).

This is the format of the equestrian events at the Olympics Games—and we enjoyed it most recently in 1976 at

Bromont outside of Montreal, with Great Britain's Princess Anne much in the limelight, Ted Coffin of the United States the individual winner and West Germany taking the team gold medal. The Games, as with most other international sports, are the ultimate goal of the avid three-day rider, although off-year competitions in national, European, Pan-American and world championships also bring out exciting talent to watch.

A Royal Role

The weight of FEI attention, both in this country and abroad, has, of course, been placed on riding competition, but the personal weight of the FEI's president, Prince Philip of Great Britain, can often be found placed on the box of a competition carriage harnessed to four Cleveland Bay horses from the Royal Mews or the stables at Windsor Castle—they together pursuing such thrills as driving 26 miles across British or European countryside through hazards, both natural and contrived, in less than three hours. This pursuit, of course, meets the demands of the "marathon" or cross-country section of driving's adaptation of the riding world's roads and tracks and steeplechase phases of their competition.

Prince Philip is generally credited with initiating the inclusion of combined driving in the FEI rules book. A lifelong horseman and polo player until arthritis in his wrist made striking the ball both difficult and painful, Prince Philip has developed a keen interest in the driving sport. But it was in his role as FEI president at the 1966 Aachen International Horse Show in West Germany that his work toward formal FEI driving rules began. There, he recalls, he was "astonished to see at least 25 four-in-hands lined up in the ring for a class." However, there was no uniformity of driving rules and frequent clashes followed between whips

and others from rival countries on either side of the Iron
Curtain, and each other, regardless of their politics. As a
result, associates urged the FEI chief to take a hand.
Through his encouragement, even as his own personal in-
volvement as a whip grew, rules for a combined driving
event were written, and formal FEI driving competition was
begun in 1969.

Winds of Change

FEI driving rules initially were written for four-in-hands
only, and remain generally the same today. But adaptations
in many countries, including the United States, now encourage singles and pairs. Changes in distances and times
are allowed and special compensations are made for pony
entries.

As we saw in the "Events" chapter, the United States enjoys several combined driving events each year, chief among
these being the Myopia Driving Event at Hamilton, Massachusetts. Variations on the theme pop up from year to
year—sometimes as special events of their own and sometimes as part of the plentiful pleasure-driving shows where
most classes are run under American Driving Society rules,
but marathons under FEI rules.

However, in spite of this willingness to accommodate and
in spite of the fine efforts to introduce newcomers to combined driving we shall read about in the next section, we are
not totally comfortable about encouraging the beginner to
jump into the combined driving swim. He must consider the
things he will be asked to accomplish with his horse and
vehicle before he entertains any thought of entering a combined driving event. Any beginner can certainly aspire to
become part of this exciting sport, but he or she should be
wary. The thrills are enormous, but there are risks to consider.

COMBINED DRIVING IN ACTION

Professionally planned and directed, with constant attention to safety, the drive put on by the Shone Establishment in the Millbrook, New York hunt country has been an excellent combined driving testing ground, and Victor and Evelyn Shone have made a special effort to provide a less strenuous three-day trip for newcomers through their novice division. They have been careful to bring the new student whips along slowly, first assigning them "on the ground" duties which allow them to observe while helping run the competition; they move from there to a Novice test. Once through this novice introduction, the whip can then look forward to competition in Elementary and Intermediate categories. ("Advanced" classification is rare in the United States, although the official FEI Advanced dressage test has been offered several times.)

The competition, regardless of category, begins with Sections #1 and #2 of Competition A. These are known as "Presentation" and "Dressage." The next phase, Competition B, or the "Marathon," is, at standard events, held on the second day. Competition C, or the "Obstacle Driving" test, follows on the third day.

Competition A

In Presentation, the entry is judged upon the cleanliness, suitability, and general condition and appearance of the entire turnout. (Woe to the careless whip whose tool kit lacks an item of required spare equipment here!) Once judged, the entry then retires to the sidelines until summoned to drive the appropriate dressage test, from memory. The FEI elementary dressage test calls for 18 different movements at the *walk, collected trot, working trot, extended trot, halt* and *back.*

The Intermediate test is more demanding still, and the Advanced test requires deviations from the forward direction while driving with one hand, and other similar intricacies. The novice dressage test introduced by Victor Shone—there are no novice tests written by FEI headquarters since novices do not drive four-in-hands—called for 16 different movements at the *walk* and *working trot, halt* and *back.*

It should be pointed out here that in the pure FEI form, scoring continues throughout its three Competitions until completion and only then is a trophy or ribbon awarded. However scores of each individual performance are posted immediately after each Competition and the cumulative standing of the competitors listed. Also the marks received during the Dressage section are presented to each entry on cards signed by the judges.

Competition B

The Marathon consists of five sections, all at different speeds. The novice course at Millbrook called for an opening trot section of 1.46 miles to be completed in 10 minutes and 28 seconds; a walk section of .26 miles in 4.18; a faster trot section of 1.47 miles in 9.36; another walk of .25 miles in 4.54, and a final trot section covering 1.45 miles in 12.24. The middle section (C) contained numerous hazards such as driving through a "tea garden" complete with tables, chairs and umbrellas; a "cordwood junction" forming a narrow path through stacks of firewood; twists through trees, a plunge into a pond and others, six in all. As in other Marathon classes, precise penalties were assigned to mistakes, from breaking the prescribed gait to exceeding the time allowed to finish each section (half penalties for being too fast). The whip, being an aid, to be carried at all times, putting it down in a penalty zone earning a penalty. A groom dismounting in a hazard earning marks against the whip. As if tipping over isn't bad enough by itself, the hazard judge to mark down 60 penalties there alone. Even in this novice competition, going off course meant elimination. And so forth. This novice test certainly proved a precise exercise in driving skill, timing ability and training. With all that was involved in this one section it is obvious that the novice who survived was a beginner no longer.

Competition C

Competition C, which is the obstacle driving test and comes last in the three days, can be conducted either on the basis of the number of obstacles knocked over, or against the clock. The first is the more popular with organizers. A course of 20 obstacles, or gates, measuring approximately 550 to 875 yards, is set up within an arena. The cones or markers which, in pairs, form the obstacles are placed for each vehicle to allow specified clearances depending upon the category—Novice (at least at Millbrook), Elementary and Intermediate. An easily-dislodged tennis or polo ball sits atop each marker or cone; if it falls, 10 faults are given. More severe marks are given for a second disobedience or a groom dismounting and whips better mind their manners and those of their horses lest they be eliminated for all sorts of prohibited activities. Ties are dissolved by the faster time through the course.

Upon completion of the obstacle competition, the entries line up by divisions—Novice, Elementary and Intermediate; and by categories—Single Pony, Single Horse, Pairs of Ponies, etc.—to receive their awards. Placings are determined by the entire effort over the three days.

The Rationale

There is a precise reasoning behind the order of the three Competitions. The Presentation is pretty obvious as ex-

40. Kellington Farm pair of Kitchener and Kingston negotiating the "splash" during the 1976 Myopia Combined Driving competition. The referee is Mrs. Oliver Appleton; the vehicle a shooting cart.

plained above. The Dressage—the second half of Competition A—"displays the freedom, regularity of paces, harmony, impulsion, suppleness, lightness, ease of movement and correct positioning of the horse on the move." The FEI rules book adds that "the competitor also will be judged on his style, accuracy and general command of his horse." Competition B—the Marathon—is designed "to test the standard of fitness and stamina of the horses and the judgment and horsemastership of the competitor." Competition C—Obstacles—is "to test the fitness, obedience and suppleness of the horses after the Marathon, and skill and competence of the competitor (driver)."

As in the case of the combined riding world, the complete picture is often sublimated to the individual parts, and in the case of the programs which compress the three days into two, the intent of the originators in Switzerland is pretty much ignored. The two-day schedules put Competitions A and C together on the first day. This takes away from Competition C (Obstacles) the initial intent—to prove that the entries have survived the grueling Marathon without lameness or weariness. It turns this third portion of the overall event into a simple test of driving skill and handiness of the horses. And it takes away something from the following day's Marathon in that the inroads of the marathon on stamina and soundness become less apparent. Lameness appearing after the horse is cooled out does not become a factor in the awarding of the prizes. However the three Competitions are driven the same way under the same rules and the course of the event remains exciting and testing.

WHEN A NOVICE?

Victor Shone designed his novice marathon course over 4.89 miles, which is a far cry from the 26 miles of the world or European championships, but he did so deliberately to encourage newcomers, not necessarily beginners. Note the distinction. Let us say that for the purposes of combined driving competition a novice is a driver of adequate experience who would like to compete against others of his level. How much experience is "adequate"? That depends, of course, on the individual, his skills and the training and manners of his horse, but when an individual has been able to go out by himself consistently, with his horse or pony under quiet and complete control, when they have handled cross-country jaunts to a picnic spot safely, when they have found the way ahead blocked and have managed the backing and turning necessary to get out of that trouble, when horse and driver have established a relationship of trust and understanding, then it might be time to consider a start in the direction of the novice division of a combined driving event.

The novice driver almost must have an understanding of harness, both fit and condition. A poor or careless fitting of any part of the harness will lead to chafes, rubs, galls and other sources of discomfort or pain to the horse. Tired and weak leather is dangerous at all times, but more so under the stresses of cross-country terrains such as side hills, steep pitches, river crossings and the like.

THE BEST VEHICLE

The two-wheeled cart is used by virtually all of the novice drivers. A few of the more experienced whips may choose a four-wheeled vehicle such as a trap, Bronson wagon and so forth, but the safest and most practical is the two-wheeled road cart. These are light, sturdy and maneuverable. Another plus for these, as we discussed earlier, is that new ones are now being made by several firms in the East. Built along traditional lines with high wooden wheels they are acceptable in the competitions where "sulky" type show or road carts are banned. And while they can cost up to $1,000 each, the risk of damaging one poses a lesser financial loss than that of damaging or ruining one of the much more valuable antiques, such as those of the "Long Island group," which are becoming increasingly difficult to find.

A SPECIAL CHALLENGE

A far cry from the pleasure driving ring and the harness classes of the breed shows, the cross-country or marathon competition is constantly challenging. In addition to the problems of moving rapidly over rough ground, up and down hill, through brooks and ponds, the cross-country course at the George Weymouth, Jr. Invitational near Chadds Ford, Pennsylvania, takes entries through three fords of the swiftly-flowing, belly-deep Brandywine River, while the Black River at Gladstone, New Jersey, and the Ipswich at Topsfield, Massachusetts, are others lying in wait on the combined driving circuit.

Contrived dumps are the choice of some course designers. Ins and outs through sheds cluttered with farm machinery are fairly familiar. Sometimes other surprises are really breath-catching. On a Vermont course once the competitors encountered a large bull calf in the middle of a woods road. The horses snorted and shied before small laughing boys drove the chained bovine out of the way. Another time a loud and lusty brass band made a frightening din under a porte-cochere through which the horses were made to pass. In the 1975 world championships at Sopot, a Baltic seashore resort in Poland, drivers were required to proceed under a pier at low tide some 75 yards before emerging onto a crowded beach where hundreds of sun-worshipers lounged on the sand in their bikinis. The pleasure driving ring was never like that!

In 1977 devotees of FEI combined driving competitions in the United States scored some notable gains. The American Driving Society established a committee to oversee combined driving events. Members of this committee visited British and European competitions, observing, and in some cases, either competing in them or serving as referees, hazard judges and the like. The inaugural program at Gladstone was an obvious success. Many of the more conventional driving competitions adopted one or several classes simulating FEI sections—mini-marathons, obstacle classes and dressage, for instance. The ADS has written driving tests designed to be used in the selection of "best" juniors, men, and women drivers.

At this writing there is little doubt that the combined event is becoming an important part of the whole driving experience in North America, even as it has grown into a well-anchored under-saddle activity. Further, a move is well under way to include combined driving in the scope of the U.S. Pony Clubs, thus exposing even more junior riders to the many thrills and happenings within the driving scheme of things.

One additional note, though this is a long way apart from the novice's status in combined driving: In 1978 the ADS established a committee to select and support (financially and otherwise) an American entry in the 1980 world championships. This would be the first-ever U.S. entry to be officially named to such an event; in effect, it would be our "national" team. An initial pledge of $50,000 has been received, but is is estimated that the eventual cost will be more like $150,000.

11

Driving the Pair

THINK OF a horse-in-harness portrait and the one that will likely pop to mind will be that of a smart pair of perfectly matched horses being driven to an elegant carriage by an impeccably turned out whip with grooms to match. This scene has certainly been a favorite of artists and photographers over the years—perhaps because two horses are easier to get on the canvas or in the lens than a four-in-hand; or, perhaps, if one horse is fascinating to artists, two are even more so.

And, if horse pairs are fascinating to the artist, they are all the more so to the already involved horseman. However, driving a pair is certainly not for the beginner, even though it is a more reachable goal than driving a tandem, for instance. There are several reasons for this—the primary one being that with a pair of horses one still has to cope with only two reins, as with a single horse, whereas the tandem demands four. As one might imagine, the handling of four reins guiding two horses calls for a skill much more difficult to achieve.

Of course, there is this to be said for the tandem: horses of different colors and heights can be made to go well to-

gether and to look attractive, whereas with a pair, everything must match if the turnout is to be pleasing to the eye.
And—sadly—in this era, matching horses are not found in
every stable, nor, indeed, in every town.

FINDING A PAIR

Practically speaking, the best way to find your pair is to buy
it already made, or at least started. There have been some
instances, of course, where pairs have been put together by
neighbors or friends; but, for the most part, these have oc-
curred within the breeds. The Morgans—with different individuals stamped so much like the next one—are prime
examples of this. So are the pony breeds. And, it is not impossible to find two Standardbreds which look and move
alike.

But, since we have been dealing with the saddle horse
turned harness horse for much of this book, we would warn
that putting two of these together on either side of the pole
with the thought that they would look like those smart
turnouts so familiar in the books and journals of the equine
world is more dream than reality. It is not impossible to
drive two such horses down the road regardless of how they
look as they go, and there can be enjoyment and benefit
gained, but the fact is that two horses unmatched in size,
color and way of going do not make a true pair.

The exception is the proof. In the 1960's, when we were
much involved in fox hunting and the exercise of the hunting horses was necessary, Kellington Farm did drive mis-
matched hunters two at a time with success and pleasure,
particularly for the lady of the house whose bad back kept
her out of the saddle. These were not smart turnouts and
we were well aware of that but it got the job done, and as a
matter of record we drove a cob-type 15.0 hands with a
rangy hunter almost 16.0 to a cutter in a public sleigh rally

and won ribbons. They were both grey and they moved somewhat alike but that was as close to a pair as they came.

So where do the pairs we now see begin? Some come from the nurseries of the various breeds but this source isn't as fruitful as one might imagine: most of the Morgan pairs, for instance, remain committed to life within the show ring. Many come from Canada where similarity among the crossbred foals is common. A few are imported from Europe. And there is a growing realization among the horse farmers in the American heartland that there is a market for pairs of lighter horses now as well as for the heavy drafters, thus the recent sales in Indiana and Iowa, and even Massachusetts, have included pairs of what are variously called "fancy teams," "commercial teams," and/or "driving pairs."

As a unit pairs are in a great minority. This is natural. Economics cannot be ignored: two horses eat twice as much as one horse, eight shoes cost twice as much as four, etc. Pair harness is much more difficult to obtain than single harness. And the logistics of working a pair are more complex than those involved with a single horse and carriage.

So far this discussion has been mostly negative since we wanted to make the beginner aware of some of the problems he must consider as he ponders a move toward pair driving. But right here we should add that the most fun we have had in all our years of driving has been with pairs. Given the right conditions there can be a great deal of pleasure in turning out a fine pair of matched horses and driving them through the countryside or in the various forms of competition.

WHICH VEHICLE?

Earlier in this book we discussed the many types of vehicles in use by the pleasure driver. Discard now any idea of a

41. The author and his wife, Daphne, behind Kingston and Kitchener—
their hackney and French coachmare crossbred pair—at the 1976
Stonybrook, Long Island, picnic drive.

two-wheeled cart for a pair. These are rare, as they always were, and require intricate harness and rigging. The "curricle" is an elegant vehicle demanding special horses and they are almost non-existent; the "Cape Cart" from South Africa is seldom seen in America. But many of the four-wheeled vehicles of American design which we discussed in chapter 3—the buggy, the surrey, many types of phaetons and traps, to name a few—can be used with a pair by the simple substitution of a pole for the shafts. Light carriage poles seem to be in almost better supply than shafts—this perhaps because there is relatively less demand for them and because they seem to have survived the years since the end of the horse and buggy era in better condition than the more fragile (in design) shafts. The simple pole with its built-on double-tree at the carriage end and a neck-yoke bar at the tip is all that it takes to convert any light carriage from single to pair use.

The more formal sporting carriages of British and European design specifically planned for a pair of horses heavier than the Morgan or the Standardbred are equipped with a splinter bar instead of a double-tree; a rigid pole and a crab (steel fixture) on the tip end, which with pole straps or chains, replaces the neck-yoke—an almost purely American device in origin. This calls for a more formal harness.

WHAT ABOUT HARNESS?

If you are going to drive two horses you will need two sets of harness, of course—one for each horse. This does add to the cost of driving a pair. Light pair harness can be found in the Amish harness shops, generally made to order since the sects do not normally drive two horses: they feel that one buggy horse can do the necessary road work and that two might be considered ostentatious. But their harness makers are tuned to the desires and dollars of the outside world and simple pair harness can be purchased.

What we wrote about buying used harness for the single horse goes double when trying to outfit a pair. Unfortunately, the whip who wants to upgrade from the basic Amish harness for pairs, must go to the dealers and the auction sales for the traditional and stylish sets of coaching-type harness, or he must have new made. Further, the harness bought on the auction block must be expected to cost almost as much to restore and rebuild as the sales price: often buyers consider they are bidding only for the hardware in the old harness, and plan to have it rebuilt completely. Thus, there isn't a great deal of choice between the cost of a rebuilt harness or a completely new one.

A PAIR FOR A PAIR

Not only is pair driving more expensive than single driving, it is more demanding. The logistics involved require a helper when putting to, and generally, when taking away from the carriage. Teamsters of old harnessed their wagon and work horses to a pole-equipped vehicle or farm machine, it is true, but those horses had been trained to back into position and stand there. This can be done today, given sufficient time and practice, but two people can handle the task of properly and safely attaching two horses to a vehicle a lot faster than one person. If the helper does nothing but lead the second horse into position and then hold the heads of the two horses while the trainer-driver does all the hitching, his or her help is most welcome. The need for this second presence continues through the whole experience of driving a pair: certainly no lady should venture off the home premises without a second person who can assist in a moment of need whether it be something as simple as a glove dropped in the road, or a stone lodged in a hoof, or the potentially more serious occurrences such as a break in harness or vehicle. One person trying to handle two horses in such a situation is hard-pressed to keep everything in place, but just a little help from a second person makes all the difference.

At Kellington Farm we try to hew to the rule that no pair of horses goes out with only one person, but it doesn't always work. We have a veteran pair of geldings which we allow out with an experienced whip alone, but it still requires two people to put those bays in the carriage and most of the time we like to have a second person there when they come back and are taken out. It could be done by one person and it has been, but the better way is with two!

HARNESSING THE PAIR

Trial and error is the method best used to harness the pair to the carriage. There are several crucial fittings which can make life a lot more pleasant, or unpleasant if done wrong. As the accompanying illustration indicates, a pair of horses is driven by a set of draft and coupling reins. The draft rein is the "straight" rein; that is, it goes from the hand part to the outside ring of the bit on each horse. The coupling rein is buckled to the draft rein and it runs to the inside ring on each of the two bits. Depending on the individual horses in the pair these reins must be adjusted very precisely in order to insure that contact will be maintained equally in the mouths of the two horses.

The traces, too, must be adjusted carefully so that each horse can do his share of the work. Quite often it will be found that the length of the traces must be varied from horse to horse, even from one side to the other of one horse, in order to keep the work load level.

Two types of breeching for pairs are in favor in this country at present. The beginner who wants to move to a pair to use on, say, the surrey he had been pulling with a single horse, and who buys a set of harness from the Amish shops, can get along very nicely with a "Boston backer" type of breeching wherein two straps run from the rings on either

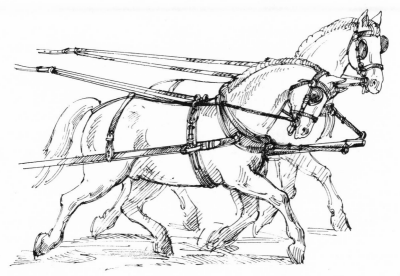

42. A pair harness in action. Compare this harness with that in Figure 14 and with Figure 43.

end of the breeching itself to a single ring placed on the end of the breast plate at the girth. This arrangement restrains the collars from moving out and away from the normal position when the weight of the carriage is applied to the pole straps. More formal harness comes with side straps running from the breeching rings to the trace buckles.

Neck or "round" collars generally are favored with a pair but in this country many of the lighter harnesses are equipped with breast collars. Strong metal "Ds" are sewn into the front of these collars to which are attached the pole straps. The neck collar arrangement includes hames, two to a collar, which are fastened at the top by a hame strap and at the bottom by a "kidney" link. This has a loose ring through which the pole strap passes; in the event of a finer harness calling for pole chains when driven by an amateur

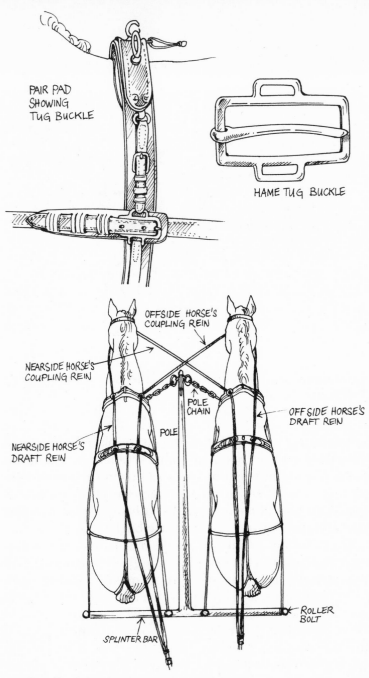

PAIR PAD
SHOWING
TUG BUCKLE

HAME TUG BUCKLE

OFFSIDE HORSE'S
COUPLING REIN

NEARSIDE HORSE'S
COUPLING REIN

POLE
CHAIN

OFFSIDE HORSE'S
DRAFT REIN

POLE

NEARSIDE HORSE'S
DRAFT REIN

ROLLER
BOLT

SPLINTER BAR

43. Details of the pair harness: an overview.

or owner, the chains pass through the loose ring and thence to loose rings in the pole head. The lighter American harnesses often have hames with hame straps top and bottom instead of the kidney link and the pole straps are passed around the entire collar.

DRIVING THE PAIR

The actual guiding and control of a pair in contrast to a single horse is not twice as hard, as one might expect—particularly if the horses are well-broken and well-matched as far as gait goes. A horse which is timid and apt to shy quickly when alone often takes comfort from his mate and becomes less of a problem. A quiet and seasoned veteran will be a calming influence on an excitable mate, although the contrary happens occasionally.

One of the major problems in driving a pair is that of keeping them together in stride and in work. Horses that may look exactly alike may not work alike at all. Horses are like people: some work hard, others do as little as they can and get away with it. Some smart horses will learn just to keep the traces taut while their mate does all the work; these are hard to detect until you see one horse all blown and sweaty at the top of a grade while his mate is breathing easily and hasn't turned a hair. Our American system of single-trees and evener, or double-trees if you prefer, makes it a little easier to catch the lazy one at his game.

However, in many cases the lagging horse is not lazy but just has a shorter stride than his mate: this, of course, would be considered a major drawback to their continued use as a pair.

As we said, pair driving is not for the beginner, but it certainly is an exciting and pleasurable part of the driving scene and something to think about as one's skills improve—if one's interest and pocketbook leans that way.

12

Restoration Hints

U N L E S S the beginning driver is an accomplished car-
penter, or cabinet-maker type with a heated work shop
filled with sophisticated wood-working and other tools, the
thought of attempting to restore an antique—or
antiquated—carriage usually fills him or her with dismay. It
needn't. Housewives, doctors and nurses, a sailing en-
thusiast whose wife has become an ardent driving
competitor—these, and many more we know, have put their
hands and their heads to the task of restoring a vehicle and
have produced a finished product as strong and attractive as
when new 75 years ago or more.

It isn't easy, but the task is pleasant and not particularly
strenuous, nor need it be very expensive. While one can
find professional services almost every step of the way, to do
it yourself, or as much of it as you can, will save a lot of
money, besides being so much more rewarding.

START WITH A MODEL

One of the first steps we recommend is that you see a restored version of the carriage you plan to work on. These

can be found in one of a number of museums open to the public. The Smithsonian Institute in Washington and the Ford Museum at Dearborn in Michigan hold extensive collections. In the Northeast, principal collections have been gathered at Shelburne in northwestern Vermont and at the Museums and Carriage House at Stony Brook in Long Island's Suffolk County. The Morven Park restoration complex in Virginia contains the collection of the late Viola Windmill, and there is a small but elegant collection on the grounds of the Broadmoor Hotel in Colorado Springs, Colorado. These are but a few of the more extensive collections. Many private collectors have impressive numbers of carriages and sleighs which can be seen by appointment. You can also visit one of the many driving shows and study the vehicles there, and perhaps talk to someone who already has restored a horse-drawn vehicle. People who have restored antique automobiles may also prove helpful. Membership in the American Driving Society and the Carriage Association of America will also be of help to the neophyte restorer through contact with others of similar interests.

SUPPLIERS

In the last few years, as enthusiasm for driving has mounted, so has the number of commercial firms and individuals who can do part or all of any required restoration. The wheelwright's shop, once a species endangered to the vanishing point, has been reborn, with shops reopening or starting from scratch across much of the country. The Amish and Mennonite sects remain a principal source of wheels, axles, boxes and assorted carriage parts and hardware both in this country and in Canada, even as they are the main sources of plain but serviceable harness. In the Northeast, drivers turn to the "Pennsylvania Dutch" enclaves, but throughout the land wherever these religious sects are found one can obtain parts and help from the artisans abundant there.

Beyond these sects are the wheelwrights and carriage builders who are now returning to these old crafts. In 1977 the Carriage Association circulated throughout its membership a long national list of such shops and individuals. Their secretary, Horace Sowles, Jr. (P.O. Box 3788, Portland, Maine 04101) might still have a few copies left or be able to tell anyone interested how one can be obtained. These shops also advertise: in *The Whip*, newsletter of the American Driving Society; *The Carriage Journal*, quarterly magazine of the Carriage Association; and *The Yankee Pedlar*, a northeastern monthly—to name only a few.

WHO DOES WHAT

The more difficult parts of a vehicle to repair are the various pieces of the running gear—the wheels, axles and their components. The professionals can fix these probably better than all but the most talented amateur craftsman. Also somewhat beyond the scope of the average home shop are the shafts which must be fitted and bent to conform to the type of vehicle or to match the unbroken shaft remaining. These, too, are available from the professionals. Most iron work above the running gear can be fixed or replaced in local blacksmithing shops. Numerous locations now handle the chore of re-tiring wheels, both in steel and in rubber. A special note: when removing wheels for any purpose be careful to label each one with its exact position—"right front," "left rear," etc. Wheels are not interchangeable. Boxes are fitted to the individual spindle (axle), thus each set is unique to the others. And you can't just go into a wheelwright's shop and order a brand new set of wheels to fit your old vehicle for the same reason.

More recently, Amish and other wheelwrights have

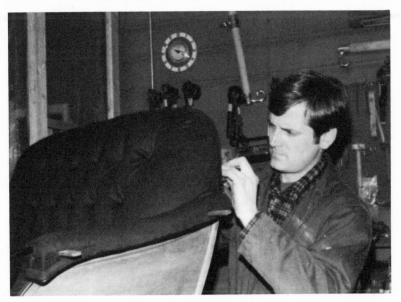

44. Refinishing in progress.

turned to using a ball-bearing arrangement which makes the task of fitting new boxes to old spindles somewhat easier, and lessens the wheel-wobbling inclinations of worn parts.

The body, seats, dashboard, fenders and over-all finish and restoration are well within the ability of any handy person. New wheels and shafts come rough and unfinished, so these will be your responsibility as well.

WHERE TO BEGIN

Regardless of whether your vehicle is painted or is natural wood, it must be taken apart as much as possible. The way we do it is label each part, putting the pieces into containers for safekeeping. Every piece should be stripped and sanded down to the bare wood. Examine each wooden piece for rot, either wet or dry; ailing and broken pieces can be replaced in home wood-working shops or by your neighborhood cabinet maker.

Patent leather dashboards found to be rough and cracked should be removed and the leather closely examined to see whether it can be repaired or must be replaced. If upholstery remains, this should be removed carefully, studied to see how it was attached, what materials were used, how the buttons were sewn in, etc. "I write notes to myself describing the methods I find," says the lady of our house—and our chief restorer.

Once the basic soundness of the vehicle has been established—the working parts either repaired or replaced, the body disassembled, stripped to bare wood and reassembled, with any replacement pieces made, if necessary—the work of the refinisher turns to the finishing.

THE FINISHING

First, coats of filler must be applied and sanded repeatedly to guarantee a smooth surface. Careful cleaning with a tack rag between coats is of utmost importance (dirt and dust are the biggest problem of the home restorer). The number of coats necessary will vary with the condition of the wood, but the goal is a perfectly smooth, mirror-like finish. All the pores, as well as the grain, must be filled. Dents and scratches will need further filling with a putty-like substance such as Nitrostan: plastic wood is not acceptable since it will crack out once the vehicle is in use.

Once the final sanding is finished, the enamel is applied—sanding between coats to maintain the desired smoothness. In the event that the restorer is working on a natural wood vehicle, spar varnish or a good urethane is used. Meanwhile, the metal parts should be sanded, prepared with an undercoating of Rustoleum or something

45. A beautifully restored Kentucky breaking cart, in this case behind the first-place winner Romansar with Maureen Zeko, owner/whip, up.

similar, and then painted in the traditional black.

As we mentioned, dust and dirt are the curse of the home restorer. Every effort should be made to work in a dust-free atmosphere: sprinkle the floor with a watering can; hang plastic sheets around the carriage; keep as much traffic out of the area as possible, particularly the children and pets. Weather extremes, particularly cold and dampness, should be avoided.

Appropriateness

The saddest sight for many carriage lovers is to see a traditional vehicle all gussied up like a circus wagon. Sporting vehicles may be bright but tradition dictates the finish of these, too: green, yellow, red, blue, etc. Striping is a very exacting task and bad striping betrays the amateur. Better to paint all the hardware—such as bolt heads, shaft clips, etc.—black than to do a poor striping job.

THE UPHOLSTERY

After the painting is completed thoughts should then turn to the upholstery. The main tool here, beyond the familiar tack hammer and shears, is a long upholsterer's needle (obtainable at upholstery shops) for doing the buttons. Traditional fabrics such as Bedford cord, wool broadcloth, melton and corduroy are the best. Some vehicles were done in leather. This is very costly today: a good grade of imitation material such as Naugahyde will suffice; however, cheaper vinyls are not satisfactory and will not be attractive. Horse hair from an old mattress is the best stuffing, but polyester makes an acceptable substitute.

If there was no old upholstery left to study on the original vehicle, a trip to a museum or to a collector will prove of great help or, as a last resort, consult a professional carriage finisher or an expert upholstery shop.

THE LEATHER WORK

If the leather dashboard is sound but "alligatored" (rough and bumpy), strip the leather carefully with a good paint remover until the leather is completely bare. Clean it carefully with alcohol; then apply coats of black enamel or Varathane to finish the restoration. The same can be done for the leather covering the fenders: however, the ideal method is to recover them with new patent leather. The main problem is to get the leather on the frame tight enough so there will be no wrinkles or buckling.

Placing new leather on the shafts is easy—if you know how. First you measure and cut, leaving about three inches more than the circumference of the shaft. Thoroughly soak the leather in water, then fit it around the shaft smoothly and tightly with your hands; the leather to be centered on the shaft with the excess leather divided equally on either side—the overage, obviously, to go to the underside. Then pull the overlaps together very tightly with clamps placed closely along the length of the leather, and hand stitch along the full length. Remove the clamps; then trim off the excess from the flaps with a very sharp knife, razor, etc. Finally, bone the cut edges with beeswax until they are smooth.

Some old carriages will have had the leather pieces on the shafts tacked on instead of sewn. This can be done, being careful to have the edges butt together the whole length of the leather. But this is not as neat a job as one sewn, nor does it last as long since the tacks can work loose. Of course those shafts reinforced on the underside with iron would be impossible to tack.

The catalogue of an Amish carriage maker in hand shows three pieces of protective leather on each shaft plus two sets of shaft straps. Again, the best way to accomplish these fine points properly is to study a completed vehicle.

Above all, don't get discouraged or give up. Parts, repairs, and professional advice are obtainable as, and if, needed. If you find you just can't "do it yourself," you can get it done elsewhere and probably not too far from your own door.

Glossary

ADS, or A.D.S.—American Driving Society

Apron—a cloth worn to keep the wearer clean, dry and warm while driving. For private driving an individual apron is usually worn. In summer a cotton or linen check with matching binding is appropriate; in winter, a heavier material lined with wool is better. The apron is made to buckle around the waist and cut long enough to almost reach the feet and wide enough to tuck in well when seated. More elaborate turnouts often have aprons attached directly to the box and rumble. *See* Box, Rug *and* Rumble.

Axle—the metal axis on which the wheels of the driving vehicle turn, the most common being the Collinge's axle. Axles, once made from solid timbers tapered down to accommodate the wheels, were then known as axle trees.

Back band—for single harness, the strap passing through the saddle to which the shaft tugs are fastened. On some harness the back band is pointed at each end, with the belly band buckled on either side to hold the back band on. *See* Tug(s).

Backstrap—the strap which joins the crupper's dock(tail)-piece to the saddle pad. Some are buckled to allow easier tail entry; others are sewn solid. *See also* text *and* Figure 14.

Bar(s)—the part of the horse's mouth on which the bit rests. *See* Bits and Bitting, Liverpool bit *and* Port.

B.D.S.—British Driving Society.

Bearing rein—the rein which, through a bridoon, connects the horse's mouth to the saddle pad and forces the head into the desired position. The driving reins are normally attached to the lower bit. There are two chief types of bearing rein: the pulley and the plain, although the overhead check is also used. *See* Bits and Bitting, Bridoon, Overhead check *and* Figures 14, 15, and 18.

Bellyband—Either as a separate band buckled onto the back band, or as one continuous strap, the belly band serves to keep the shafts securely in position. This is important both for balance on the road and for security when loading the two-wheeled cart. *See* Figure 14.

Bit(s) and Bitting—the mouthpiece attached to the horse's bridle which allows the driver to exert pressure on the horse's mouth—both on the tongue and at the bars. The severity of this pressure depends on the particular variation of bit and bitting used. Some of the most popular pleasure driving bits are the Wilson snaffle, the Liverpool, the Buxton, and the Elbow. *See* Bar, Curb bit, Liverpool bit, Port and Snaffle. *See also* text *and* Figure 16.

Blinders—*See* Blinkers.

Blinkers—leather-covered metal plates attached to the cheek-pieces of the bridle to prevent the horse from seeing behind himself. Also known as blinders, and in England as winkers, they can be one of several shapes, but as with other pieces of harness must fit properly.

Boot—in earlier days, the uncovered box-shaped projections slung along the coach between the front and rear wheels; in later days, the somewhat larger and lidded box behind many coaches, sometimes even accommodating passengers.

Box—the seat from which the driving is done. The seat itself is flat, though the driver actually sits at a slight slope, usually achieved by a special pillow or by a special piece built onto the seat. The proper angle is important to the driver's control of the horse, allowing his feet adequate purchase.

Branches—the sides of a curb bit to which the mouthpiece is fixed and the reins buckled.

Break, or Brake—an open four-wheeled vehicle. *See also* Roof-seat break.

Breaking cart—for the single horse, a sturdy two-wheeled, long-shafted vehicle. It should be low to the ground with easy step-on, step-off access for the trainer/driver. *See also* text *and* Figures 28 and 45.

Breeching—the harness apparatus by which the horse holds back the vehicle when there is no brake. *See also* Figures 14 and 21.

Bridle—a leather headpiece which accommodates the blinkers and bit, and when wanted, bearing reins. As with other pieces of harness, its care is important. *See also* Figure 17.

Bridoon—a snaffle bit positioned slightly above the regular bit.

Buckboard—a springless four-wheeled vehicle with the seats built above and on one or more boards stretched from the front to the rear axles.

Buggy—a light four-wheeled carriage of many varieties, but generally hung on two elliptic or semi-elliptic springs and a perch. *See* Springing *and* Perch. *See also* text *and* Figure 10.

CAA, or C.A.A.—Carriage Association of America.

Carriage—technically speaking, this is the part now more commonly called the under-carriage or chassis. More broadly, a carriage is taken to be almost any of the more elegant four-wheeled family driving vehicles. They can be either open or closed.

Cart—generally named after the region from which it came, or its builder, or the purpose to which it was put—there are numerous varieties. They can be either two-wheeled or four-wheeled; however, they are always open and considerably simpler than the open carriages. *See* Dog cart.

Checkrein—*See* Bearing rein.

Collar—the padded harness which goes around the horse's neck accommodating the hames to which the traces are attached. The collar can take several forms: the round and the open breast collar being the most usual. *See also* Figures 14, 18, 19, and 31, *and* Hames and Traces.

Combined driving—driving competition under the auspices of the Fédération Équestre Internationale which incorporates tests in presentation and dressage with marathon and obstacle course events. *See* Marathon and Presentation.

Crab—the steel hook and cross-head at the end of the pole to which a team's main and lead bars are hooked. *See* Figure 43.

Crupper—the harness piece that secures the saddle pad from the rear. The dock(tail)-piece runs under the tail and attaches to the saddle through the backstrap. *See* Figures 14 and 21. Since the under-tail area is sensitive it is important that the dock-piece be kept soft.   •

Curb bit—a bit that consists of two side pieces (branches) and a crosspiece (mouthpiece). It comes in many varieties, one of the most popular for driving being the Liverpool. The severity of action depends on where the reins are attached, or whether a curb chain is used and of course on the driver. *See* Bits and Bitting, Curb chain, Liverpool bit *and* Figures 16 *and* 14.

Curb chain—a small chain attached to the hooks on the eyes of a curb bit and lying under and behind the horse's mouth in the chin groove. When properly adjusted it allows more control of the pulling horse.

Cut-under—a type of vehicle construction allowing an arch into which the wheels can turn. *See* Lock *and* Figure 37.

Dee—a metal fitting, usually D-shaped, through which various parts of the harness pass.

Dog cart—a popular general purpose vehicle most often seen in its two-wheeled, single-harness version. It features back to back seats, each accommodating two and with an adjustable foot rest for the rear passengers. Some were built high enough to allow ventilated quarters for hunting dogs below the seats, thus the name. *See also* Figure 7.

Drag—a private sporting coach.

Driving reins—the reins by which the whip directs the horse or team. Russet leather is preferable; the dye from black reins could come off. The width of the reins is a matter of choice; many women find seven-eighths-of-an-inch reins comfortable, some men prefer a little wider rein. Wide reins can be hard to handle and too narrow reins may be hard to hold if there is a sudden pull or if wet. Reins that are too short are dangerous, as a fast pull could wrest them from the whip's grip; too long and they could get tangled in the whip's feet.

Elliptic springs—*See* Springing.

FEI, or F.E.I.—Fédération Équestre Internationale. *See also* Combined driving.

Four-in-hand—a popular term for a four-horse team.

Full lock—*See* Lock.

Gig—a light, rather elegant two-wheeler with a forward-facing seat generally for two. *See* Figure 8.

Governess, or tub, cart—a sturdy, low-slung two-wheeled cart loaded through a door from the rear (*See* Figure 38). With relatively high sides all round, and a secure door, it makes an ideal vehicle for young children. However, the longitudinally-placed seats, with little foot-purchase, make handling anything but a well-mannered pony difficult.

Hames—the steel arms fitted to the horse's collar. The reins pass on to the horse's mouth through an eye on each side at the top of the hames, while the traces are indirectly connected to a ring on either side of the hames towards the base of the collar. Properly fitted hames are extremely important to successful harnessing. *See* Figures 14, 19 and 3.

Jog cart—a light, two-wheeled vehicle usually made with a slotted bottom; used for exercising horses. It accommodates one or two people facing forward.

Leader(s)—the two forward horses in a team; the near leader being the left-hand horse, the off leader the right-hand. *See also* Wheeler.

Lead rein—the rein of a tandem, unicorn or team which passes from the leader to the coachman, or whip, through terrets on the harness of the intervening horse or horses. *See* Figures 31, 38 and 39.

Liverpool bit—a curb bit with five degrees of severity, the Liverpool is one of the most popular pleasure driving bits. The rein can be attached to the rings, to the branches just below the mouthpiece or to any of the three bar positions; the lower the position, the more pressure. *See also* text *and* Figure 16.

Lock—the amount of a vehicle's turning ability. Depending on the design of the vehicle, the front wheels may or may not be able to turn freely. When the body is low slung the wheels will soon run into the body; when the body has a cut-under arch, more freedom is allowed; when the perch is high enough a "full lock" can be achieved. Full lock is obviously important when trying to maneuver in tight places. *See* Cut-under, Perch.

Longeing—a training exercise to teach the horse maneuverability and discipline. *See also* text *and* Figure 27.

Long lining—a training exercise to help prepare the horse to be directed by reining from the rear rather than by the usual more immediate riding aids. *See also* text *and* Figure 26.

Marathon—an organized competitive drive over a set course at a standard time for all. The ordinary marathon is chiefly a test of fitness and suitability. The marathons of the FEI combined driving events are considerably more rigorous for horse, driver and vehicle. They have much stricter specifications, a more difficult course and a more demanding time schedule.

Near side—the left side of the horse or team. This term derived from the fact that the wagoner always walked on the left so the left side of the horse was always his "near" side. *See also* Off side.

Off side—the right side of the horse or team.

Overhead check—a type of bearing rein used especially for racing horses to keep their heads high and the breathing freer. *See* Figure 15.

Pacer—A type of horse distinguished by his leg action and often seen at trotting races driven to a sulky. Pacers move in lateral two-time; trotters move in diagonal two-time.

Pad—the small lightweight "saddle" used with pair and team harness. The pad can be much lighter and less sturdy than the saddle used for single horse harness because no weight is born directly on the horses' backs. *See* Saddle *and* Figures 14 and 18.

Perch, or Reach—the longitudinal member between the front and rear axle serving as the foundation around which the undercarriage of many vehicles is built. The elliptic spring allowed carriages to be built without a perch: this allows a lighter vehicle with a better lock. However, carriages without perches absorb any heavy vibrations on the springs, sometimes causing the pole to bounce up and strike the horses: a perch helps to steady the pole. As a compromise, many carriages feature a light perch plus two transverse elliptic springs. *See also* Springing *and* Figures 10 and 11.

Phaeton—a now almost all-encompassing term covering a wide range of four-wheeled open carriages designed to be driven from a forward seat. There were once phaetons of almost every size, shape and function, and many remain today. *See also* text and Figures 13 and 3.

Pole—a wooden member with metal fittings to which the horses for pair driving are hitched on either side. It is through the pole that the vehicle is steered and braked, if no brake is available. The size and position of the pole is very important: if the pole is too long, the pole chains hitched to the horse will lie almost parallel to the pole and not do their job; if they are too short, they will pull the horses' collars sideways. If the pole is too low, a horse may get his inside leg tangled in it. *See also* Figures 42, 43, 30 and 41.

Port—an arch in a bit's mouthpiece into which the tongue fits. This allows the tongue some room while the mouthpiece on either side of the port acts on the bars of the horse's mouth. Some horses prefer this to a straight mouthpiece; however, high ports can be too severe if not handled correctly. A melton port, for example, is higher than a Cambridge port, but not as high as a half-port. *See* Bar(s).

Presentation—a competition comparable to the fitting and showing class in a non-harness show. Judged at the halt in the dressage area, points are awarded based equally on the driver, the grooms, the horse or horses, the vehicle and the general appearance.

Putting to—attaching the harnessed horse or horses to the vehicle. *See also* text *and* Figures 19–24.

Quadrem—four horses harnessed one in front of the other.

Randem—three horses harnessed one in front of the other.

Reach—*See* Perch.

Rein(s)—*See* Bearing reins, Driving reins, Lead reins and Overhead check. *See also* text *and* Figures 14, 15 and 18.

Roadster—a type of horse originally bred in England and to which the modern Hackneys owe their heritage.

Roof seat—a seat on top of the roof of a driving vehicle.

Roof-seat break—a roof-seated, open sporting vehicle drawn by a pair or four-in-hand. *See also* text *and* Figures 31 and 30.

Rug—a throw used by some whips in preference to an apron. In summer, a light cotton or linen bound check is adequate; in winter, a darker and heavier waterproofed and wool-lined rug is more practical. The rug should be large enough to tuck in well around the user's lap and long enough to reach from the waist to the floor. Rugs will, of course, need to be available for the passengers as well as the whip. *See* Apron.

Rumble—the rearmost coach seat.

Saddle—a well-built, padded flat leather piece placed on the harness horse's back to act as the central harness anchor. Saddles are usually narrow, varying in relation to the work required. They have well-stuffed panels down each side and a girth strap on each side to which a small girth is buckled. The back band which carries the shaft tugs is passed through a slit between the saddle seat and lining. A bearing rein hook is fastened at the front and a crupper dee at the rear. A saddle is always used in preference to the plainer pad whenever the horse will have to take part of the vehicle's weight on his back, and must fit well. *See* Back band, Pad, text *and* Figures 14, 18, 19–24.

Shaft(s)—the two longitudinal timbers between which the single-harness horse is harnessed. With the two-wheeled vehicle, the shafts provide both the balance and the steering. With four-wheeled vehicles and sleighs, the shafts prevent the vehicle from running up on the horse and also aid in the steering. *See* Figure 14.

Shows and Showing—now an important part of the summer driving scene with numerous events held for private driving turnouts. At the larger shows, the entries are sometimes divided into hackney and non-hackney types, and sometimes split even further into two height sections. Several factors enter into the judge's decision: suitability of horse to vehicle; the fit and condition of the harness; the condition of the vehicle and its appointments; the horse's conformation and way of going (a straight-ahead mover who covers plenty of ground with each stride will get the nod over the one with just showy action); the horse's spirit and manageability. The dress of the whip, passengers and grooms are also factors. At some shows, marathon and obstacle-course events are included.

Side check—*See* Reins.

Single, or swingle, tree—the bar sometimes used to transmit the draft, or pull, from the traces to the vehicle. There are various methods used to connect the single-tree with the vehicle, usually to the splinter bar but sometimes directly to a vehicle fitting or, through chains, to slots by the springs: the choice is usually determined by the vehicle itself and the use to which it will be put. A single-tree allows the horse more mobility of action than does a solid trace attachment and results in a more comfortable ride for both horse and vehicle. *See* Splinter bar.

Snaffle—a bit with a mouthpiece which may be straight but is usually jointed and to which the reins are attached through rings fixed directly or indirectly to the mouthpiece. *See* Bits *and* Figure 16.

Splinter bar—the stiff bar at the front of the vehicle by which it is drawn (*see* Figure 43). Designs for a movable splinter bar making use of the single-tree action theory allow the traces to give with the alternating forward motion of the horse's shoulders. *See* Single-tree.

Springing—the various methods of carriage suspension. The earliest springing was by leather braces, the body of the vehicle hung on straps attached to four solid pillars on the undercarriage. Telegraph springs, a laterrefinement, were a combination of four double-elbow springs, two running laterally and two fore-and-aft; the lateral springs fixed at their centers to the body of the vehicle, the longitudinal springs joined to the lateral springs and to the axles. Later, whip, then cee, springs held the carriage to the undercarriage. In the early 1880's, the elliptic spring—with its upper spring joined to the vehicle and the lower to the axle—freed the vehicle from the necessity of a perch, thus allowing a ligher and more elegant vehicle. *See* Lock and Perch. *See also* the text *and* Figure 11.

Stoneboat—the heavy stone weight pulled by draft and harness horses in pulling competitions, the weight gradually increasing as the competition progresses.

Sulky—now a low single-seat vehicle built of steel with pneumatic-tires used for trotting and pacing races. Sulkies were once built on a high framework above large wheels and so named, the story goes, due to the solitary perch of the driver. *See* Figure 5.

Surrey—a four-wheeled vehicle with two identical forward-facing seats placed one behind another in a shallow box-shaped body. Some surreys feature a fringed canopy; others a fold-back top. *See also* text *and* Figure 12.

Swingle-tree—*See* Single-tree.

Tandem—two horses harnessed one in front of the other; the rear horse (wheeler) put to the shafts and the leader harnessed in front of him.

Team—a group of horses pulling together through an endless variety of hitches depending on the number involved and the use to which the team will be put. There have been as many as one hundred horses harnessed in one hitch, and maybe more, but the privately owned and driven team is usually limited to a four-in-hand and more usually a pair. *See* Four-in-hand.

Telegraph springs—*See* Springing.

Terret—the ring on the hames, pad or saddle through which the rein passes. *See* Figure 14.

Traces—the leather bands by which the draft is transmitted from the horse's collar to the vehicle. Most traces are made of two layers of leather sewn with two or four rows of stitches, though the best quality traces have a third layer of leather between the two outer layers; this rounded trace is less apt to rub the horse's side. Traces for private driving are usually made with a point to buckle into the collar hame tug buckle where it can be adjusted for length. *See also* Figures 14, 18, 19–24.

Trandem—three horses abreast harnessed with two poles.

Trap—a vehicle, at least in America, that featured a divided front seat that could be folded forward to allow access to the rear seat. Designed to seat four people, it could be fitted with a canopy.

Trotter—using a diagonal two-beat motion, trotters are raced under light harness put to a sulky.

Tug(s)—a strong buckle-topped, oval-shaped band made of two or three layers of stitched leather through which the shafts on the single-horse harness pass. The buckle is fastened to the back band which is attached, in turn, to the saddle. It is the tugs that keep the vehicle from tipping up or down once the bellyband is fastened. In pair or team driving the tug is the part of the harness by which the traces are attached to the hames. *See also* Figures 14, 42 and 43.

Unicorn—a team of three, made up by two wheelers and a leader. *See* Leader *and* Wheeler.

Wheeler—one of the pair nearest the vehicle when a four-in-hand is driven; the two nearest in the unicorn team; or the rear horse in the tandem hitch, etc.

Whip, a—the hand-held aid used by *the* whip to create the necessary impulsion and to correct certain faults in way of going. Whips vary in length and type depending on the purpose they will be put to and the vehicle being driven. However, all whips should be well made of good supple wood and well balanced. For use of the whip, *see* text *and* Figure 29.

Whip, the—the person who drives.

Whipple tree—*See* Single-tree.

Whip reel—a holder for the whip when not in use. Whips not hung in a reel are apt to warp, and the thong apt to curve, making the whip hard to handle.

Wilson snaffle—*See* Snaffle, Bits *and* Figure 16.

NOTE: No attempt has been made to include all driving vehicle types or driving horse breeds in this glossary—nor all training techniques. See the index for the vehicles and breeds discussed in this book, and for the handling and training techniques covered.

Equipment Roster

Cart or Carriage
Single-horse harness
  Bridle and Bit
  Saddle–Crupper–Backstrap–Bellyband combination
  Breeching
  Reins (driving and bearing)
  Traces
Training aids
  Longe line
  Long lines
  Whip (long)
  Breaking cart, if possible (especially if horse is to be owner-trained)
Driving whip and whip reel
Driving cushion, if needed
Leather and metal polishes; saddle soap
Tool kit (for harness repair on the road)
Apron or rug for Whip; protective covering for passengers as desired
Appropriate costume as occasion requires, including shoes with good purchase
The horse, of course!

NOTE: Detailed specifications for the above required equipment can be found in the text and glossary. See Index for specific items.

Driving Clubs

American Driving Society, 339 Warburton Ave., Hastings-on-Hudson, NY 10706

Carriage Association of America, PO Box 3788, Portland, ME., 04101

California Carriage Foundation, c/o Mrs. Judson Wright, Penryn, CA. 95663

Mid-Hudson Driving Club, c/o Mrs. Victor Shone, Nine Partners Lane, Millbrook, NY 12545

Hunterdon Horse & Pony Club, RD Box 116A, Pittstown, NJ. 08867

Boots & Saddles Club, RD #2, Allentown, PA., 18103

Columbia County Coaching Society, c/o Mrs. Thomas Kelly, Kinderhook, NY 12106

New England Region, Carriage Association of America (NER-CAA), c/o Jerry T. Ballantine, North Berwick, ME. 03906

Pittsford Carriage Association, Pittsford, NY 14534

Mid-American Coaching Society, 8583 Sherman Rd., Chesterland, OH 44026

American Tandem Club, Box 1407, Middleburg, VA., 22117

Bibliography

This list of books on driving includes several that are out of print but which may be found in some libraries and museums. Those marked with an asterisk may be ordered from the Carriage Association of America, PO Box 3788, Portland, Maine 04101.

1. Beaufort, Duke of, *Driving*, Longman's Green & Co., London, 1890
2. Canadian Horse Council, *Manual of Basic Driving*.
3. Condor, Allan A., *Training the Driving Pony**
4. Faudel-Phillips, Maj. H., *The Driving Book**
5. Ganton, Doris L., *Breaking and Training the Driving Horse**
6. Garland, *The Private Stable* (reprint), North River Press, Croton-on-Hudson, N.Y. 1978
7. Ryder, Tom, *On The Box Seat*, 3rd edition*
8. Underhill, Francis T., *Driving for Pleasure*, D. Appleton & Co., New York, 1897
9. Walrond, Sallie, *Encyclopedia of Driving*, Horse Drawn Carriages, Ltd., 1974*
10. Walrond, Sallie, *A Guide to Driving Horses*, Thomas Nelson & Sons, Ltd., London, 1971*
11. Ware, Francis M., *Driving*, Wm. Heinemann, London, 1904

Two very fine sources of information on vehicles are the catalogues of the Suffolk Museum at Stony Brook, L.I. and the Shelburne (Vt.) Museum.

Index